A BODY IN THE CHAPEL

Ipswich, 1919: On her way to teach Sunday School, Margaret Preston finds a badly injured man unconscious at the chapel gate. She and her widowed father, Reverend Preston, take him in and call the doctor. When the stranger regains consciousness, he tells them he has lost his memory, not knowing who he is or how he came to be there. As he and Margaret grow closer, their fondness for one another increases. But she is already being courted by another man...

PHILIPPA CAREY

◆

A BODY IN THE CHAPEL

Complete and Unabridged

LINFORD
Leicester

First published in Great Britain in 2018

First Linford Edition
published 2021

Copyright © 2018 by DC Thomson & Co. Ltd.,
and Philippa Carey

A catalogue record for this book is available
from the British Library.

ISBN 978–1–4448–4725–3

Published by
Ulverscroft Limited
Anstey, Leicestershire

Set by Words & Graphics Ltd.
Anstey, Leicestershire
Printed and bound in Great Britain by
TJ Books Ltd., Padstow, Cornwall

This book is printed on acid-free paper

Shock Discovery

Margaret's hand flew to her mouth. Her eyes widened, her pulse raced and she squeaked in fright.

She turned and ran the short distance home, throwing the front door open as she went.

'Father! Father! Come quickly, there's a dead man in the entrance to the chapel!'

A chair scraped across the floor of the dining-room and the Reverend Preston appeared in his shirt sleeves and waistcoat at the dining-room door, with a napkin still tucked into his collar.

'What's that you say, Margaret? A dead man?'

'Yes, yes, a dead man,' Margaret gasped, 'at the chapel door, come quickly.'

She turned and ran back to where she had found the man sprawled on the ground with blood from his head staining the chapel doorstep.

The Reverend tossed his napkin on to the hall table and hurried after her.

At the chapel he kneeled down and felt the pulse at the man's wrist as Margaret hovered nearby.

A Race for Help

It was the flashing light that had awoken her. Last night had been warm and rather sultry, so she had left the windows open to let the night air circulate. Now there was a slight breeze that ruffled the curtains and let the rising sun flicker through a gap.

The light fell on the face of Margaret Preston, twenty years old and only child of widowed Methodist minister, the Reverend Preston.

She opened her dark-brown eyes and then immediately shut them again as she was dazzled by the sun. Well, the weather forecast was correct, she thought. It looked like it was going to be another warm sunny day.

Margaret lay there for a few minutes more, listening to the birds outside and thinking ahead to this morning's Sunday school class.

Yesterday she had repaired some of the

schoolbook covers which were getting worn due to heavy use. She reminded herself to take the mended books back to the chapel schoolroom this morning.

If she did it before her breakfast, she could put the books in their places before the usual slight chaos of the children arriving.

Margaret pushed the bedclothes back and stretched languidly before taking the dressing-gown from the chair next to the bed and putting her feet into her slippers. She crossed to the door and padded down the hall to the bathroom.

It was 1919, six years now since they had come here to Ipswich and it was almost time to move on again.

As she brushed her teeth, Margaret mused that it was both an advantage and disadvantage of the Methodist church, the way it moved its ministers around, usually every three years.

On the one hand, you didn't get stuck somewhere you didn't like for very long, but on the other hand, although you might sometimes be able to extend your stay, as they had done here, you would still have to move eventually.

However, Father said Cambridge was an interesting town with lots to see and do, so she was looking forward to the move.

She went back to her room and tossed a light cotton summer dress over her head before smoothing it down over her hips.

It was cream with a small brown flower pattern, complementing her shining hair that was cut into a modern style. They may be living in the provinces, but that didn't preclude finding a good hairdresser who knew how fashions had changed during the war.

Margaret walked down the stairs and in the entrance hallway met her father's housekeeper, who was coming from the kitchen and taking breakfast things to the dining-room.

'Good morning, Mrs Hodges. I'm going to take the repaired books to the schoolroom before the children arrive, then I'll be back straightaway for breakfast.'

Mrs Hodges was in her mid-forties and getting slightly portly, rather like the Reverend Preston, due in both cases to Mrs Hodges's excellent cooking.

She smiled at Margaret in passing.

'Don't be long, dear, or else your porridge will get cold.'

Margaret went into the parlour, picked up the pile of books under one arm and went back into the hall to take the big chapel key from its hook beside the front door. She pulled the front door of the manse open and walked down the three stone steps into the small front garden. Margaret paused for a moment to take a deep breath of the cool fresh morning air. The street was quiet except for the birdsong and a couple of children already playing hopscotch further down the road. Looking up, she saw that the sky was blue and cloudless and she smiled in anticipation of another lovely summer day.

The chapel was only next door and set back slightly from the road. It had a wrought-iron fence along the front on top of the low brick boundary wall which surrounded the graveyard.

Both the house and the chapel had been built together about fifty years ago of red brick in a substantial style. The schoolroom was just inside the chapel to the left of the entrance lobby.

Margaret turned along the street and walked the few steps to the open gate leading into the chapel grounds. She was thinking about the class later that morning.

About to walk through the gate, she stopped suddenly. There was a man sprawled on the low steps just inside the gate. She stepped forward cautiously, crouching a little and looking from the side, in order to see his face.

His eyes were closed, he wasn't moving and his black hair fell over his face, but she could see blood on the step under his head.

She quickly put the books down beside the path and knelt next to him, reaching out to feel his outstretched wrist with her hand. It was cold. He must be dead.

Margaret raced back home to fetch her father. When they returned to the chapel he kneeled down to feel the pulse at the man's wrist. Margaret hovered nearby and Mrs Hodges arrived as well to see what was going on.

'He's not dead, he's still alive; but the pulse is weak and he's very cold. He also reeks of beer,' her father said, shaking his head, 'so he probably had too much, fell over and banged his head.

'Margaret, run over to the surgery and ask the doctor to come at once while Mrs Hodges and I carry him into the house.'

Margaret darted off down the street, anxiety lending wings to her feet. The doctor's surgery was only two streets away and would be closed on a Sunday morning, but there was always someone on call for emergencies.

In all probability the doctor on call was Dr Ian Gordon, that being the lot of the junior doctor in the practice. He was courting Margaret and would not normally have expected to see her until the church service that afternoon.

A Night to Remember

Major The Honourable James Radfield, twenty-four years of age, lately released from the Suffolk Regiment, pushed open the door of the function room at the Rose and Crown public house.

He was greeted loudly by many men and by a fug of smoke from their cigarettes and pipes.

It was a reunion of men who had joined the army more or less together as B Company at the start of the Great War, and who were still alive at the end.

After one of the first big battles of trench warfare, where so many of their comrades died, they had made a pact: that whoever was left at the end would meet up after the war and drink to the memory of the missing.

There were 222 men who had started that battle and so they agreed they would meet up 222 days from the end of the war, whenever that came.

There were now only just over 30 of those originals left, and half of those 30 had been injured one way or another.

Even some of the apparently fit ones had internal scars, invisible mental wounds, that didn't show on their skin.

A mixture of all ranks, they were now close-knit friends, irrespective of their original station in life, drawn together by their shared traumatic experiences.

James had started the war as a brand-new Second Lieutenant and had risen to major by a combination of competence and the need to fill dead men's shoes.

He considered himself lucky to have got through with only a few flesh wounds.

'Major Radfield, very good to see you, sir,' one of his sergeants said, shaking James's hand and clapping him on the back.

It was a familiarity that would have drawn a reprimand during the war, but times had changed.

'I was just buying another round, so tell us what you'll have.'

'Thank you, Sergeant, I'll have a pint

of black and tan,' James replied. 'Has everyone been able to get here?'

'Well, sir, now we're only missing Perkins and Jones, and Perkins was always late for everything if you weren't behind him.'

James looked around the room, noting how relaxed and animated all the men seemed to be, with the exception of two sitting in a far corner who looked glum. James remembered them; they had always been troublemakers and miseries. Life in the trenches had been wretched and boring for everybody, when it wasn't downright terrifying, but those two had made an art of it.

James wondered why they had come, since they had hated the army so much. However, they were survivors, and just as entitled to be there as everybody else.

Lance Corporal Benson and Private Wright, he recalled.

No, that wasn't it. Private Benson, not Lance Corporal. James remembered that Benson had been demoted back to private for petty theft over a year ago, just before he was badly injured and sent home.

It explained why the pair of them were sitting on their own in the corner, instead of being welcomed by the others.

When Benson had been invalided out, James had been grateful to see the back of him, even if the man was badly injured.

An officer had to remain impartial and even-handed, but even so, he would have been happy not to see either of those two reprobates ever again.

As the evening wore on, the noise grew louder, the cigarette and pipe smoke got thicker and, inevitably in the crowd, beer got spilled, some of it on to James's jacket. It was not the sort of thing he worried about at a time like this.

Towards the end of the evening, he stood up, rapped a glass on the wooden table and called for quiet.

'Men, men, quiet now, I need to talk to you all before you leave.'

He paused as the hum of conversation died down and they all gave him their attention.

'I know it's not closing time yet, but some of you need to catch trains home and I want to say a word while you're all still here.

'We didn't all start the war together – some of you didn't join B Company until just before the battle of Le Cateau, where so many of our comrades died – but we all finished the war together.

'Since 1914 we've been together through thick and thin and since that first big battle we've lost even more friends and comrades along the way.'

He paused.

'I was lucky not to be injured worse than I was and I was doubly lucky to get dragged back to our lines by some of you. Many of you were not so lucky in your injuries, but at least you are here, for which your loved ones will be thankful.

'We are here to remember those who never came back, so raise your glasses and we'll drink to the memory of our missing comrades.'

James raised his glass as did the others.

'To missing comrades,' they all murmured.

'Now,' James said, placing his glass back on the table. 'We have to look to the future and make the best of what we have, even if it wasn't what we expected five years ago. We owe this to those who haven't come home.

'I know some of you have gone back to your old jobs but some of you can't because of your injuries and for some others the work has changed.

'You all know that my father has an estate that I manage for him just south of Newmarket. It isn't so very far away by train, and it has several farms.

'I think we've all helped one another at some time. So if any of you need a job, able-bodied or not, you should call on me and I'll find a place for you. We'll find work that you're capable of, but it's not charity.

'You'll have to work as hard as anyone else but you won't go hungry, either. You're all good men and I won't have any of you feeling desperate for lack of

14

money.'

James took out his card case.

'I'll leave my visiting cards here on the table so you can be sure of where to find me if you need to. Get the train to Dullingham, walk to the house and ask for the estate steward.

'Show him my card and we'll find you work and somewhere to stay. Don't let pride make you go hungry.'

There were a number of comments around the table and the table vibrated noisily as many men pounded it with their hands in appreciation.

Not very long afterwards, some of the men were putting their coats on, saying their farewells and leaving in ones and twos.

'Which way are you going, sir?' the sergeant asked James.

'I've just got a short walk down to the Lion Hotel, where I'm staying the night, but first I must go to the gents or I might need to stop on the way!' James laughed.

'I'll say goodnight in that case, sir, as I've got to get the last train and I must

15

get going right now.'

'Ah, yes, I remember that train doesn't go beyond Bury St Edmunds, which is why I'm staying the night and leaving in the morning.

'It was good to see you again, Sergeant, take care,' James said.

They shook hands before James went through the back door to the gents' cloakroom.

When he came back, the room was empty except for the staff clearing up and he was the last to leave. He pushed open the door to the street and breathed deeply of the fresh air.

He started walking slowly down the road towards the Lion Hotel in the centre of town.

James was enjoying the warm night air and thinking of the men who had been reunited that evening.

The war was over now, the evening quiet and James was not a man to be frightened of shadows, so he paid no attention to the quiet footsteps behind him.

Then he was suddenly struck by a blow to the back of his head and everything went black.

Good Samaritan

Margaret hurried back to the manse with the doctor. By now the injured man had been moved on to the sofa in the parlour. There was a cushion and towel under his head and a blanket over him. Mrs Hodges was holding his chilled hands in her warm ones.

The doctor put his bag down on the carpet and knelt to examine the man. Margaret stood there watching, breathing hard and rather flushed from rushing to and from the doctor's surgery.

She studied the injured man. He was very tall and his feet hung over the end of the sofa. His glossy black hair had been pushed back to reveal a bloodied cut across his forehead.

She found him rather handsome, although the stubble on his jaw, a very pale face and the nasty gash on his temple were doing him no favours.

'Mrs Hodges,' the doctor said, 'would

you fetch me a bowl of warm water and a small towel as well, please?'

Leaving the doctor to examine the injured man, Margaret went with her father to the dining-room where an unfinished breakfast was still on the table.

'While we were waiting for the doctor, I looked for a wallet to see who the man might be,' her father said, 'but it was missing. His pockets had nothing but an empty card case and a handkerchief monogrammed with a 'J'.

'At first I thought his injuries were another example of the evils of too much alcohol. Now I suspect he was attacked and robbed. Perhaps he had had too much to drink and that made him an easy target.'

'That's terrible,' Margaret said. 'What kind of person would injure a man like that, rob him and then just leave him? If it hadn't been Sunday today, he could have been there for ages before he was found. He could have died!'

'There are a lot of desperate men

about at the moment, men who came back from the war and couldn't get their old job back for one reason or another.

'I agree with you, though, and wonder how someone could sink so low. On the other hand I don't suppose we can expect a robber to bandage his victims, can we?

'I also noticed that the man's clothing and shoes are of a rather fine quality. The label in the jacket is from a tailor in Savile Row in London, so it might have been a fat wallet. Now, I have to wonder what a wealthy man is doing in this part of town on foot and at night? I suppose we might find out when he wakes up.'

Just then, the doctor entered the room with his bag in his hand and Margaret and her father turned to face him.

'He's had two blows to the head,' Dr Gordon said, putting his bag on a chair. 'One on the back and one on the front. I would hazard a guess that someone hit him from behind and then he fell and hit his forehead on the ground.

'If you trip, you instinctively put your

hands out to break your fall, but if he was already unconscious when he fell, he wouldn't have done that. As a result his head would have hit the ground hard and, with a previous blow to the back of his head, he may be unconscious for a while yet.' He shrugged.

'He was lucky not to break his nose. I don't think he's cracked his skull, but he's lost quite a bit of blood as can happen with head wounds, but otherwise there's nothing obviously amiss.

'I've put a temporary bandage around his head. When I get back to the surgery I'll telephone the hospital and get them to send an ambulance for him. I'll go now and leave you to your breakfast.'

The doctor smiled, picked up his bag and turned to leave, putting his hand on the doorknob.

'Will you join us for some breakfast or do you need to make the call urgently?' the Reverend asked.

'I've already had breakfast but I wouldn't say no to a quick cup of tea. A few minutes more won't make much difference to the patient.'

The young doctor placed his bag on the floor and pulled out an empty chair next to Margaret.

'Besides, it's a chance to chat to Margaret, isn't it?' the Reverend said, lifting an eyebrow.

'Father! You're embarrassing me!'

'Come along now, it's not as if the two of you haven't been stepping out together for quite some time, is it?' the Reverend said with a grin.

He turned to the doctor.

'Ian, does your patient need to be in the hospital or will they just put him in a bed until he wakes up?'

The doctor looked up from the cup of tea that Margaret had just poured for him.

'As you say, they'll clean his wounds, put him in a bed and let him sleep it off. There's not really much else that can be done for him. He doesn't need stitches in the cuts, they're not deep enough, and they've stopped bleeding already.'

He took another sip of tea.

'He'll have some big lumps and bruising but there's not much to do about them apart from a cold cloth to reduce the swelling. His pulse is good and he'll soon warm up now. No doubt he will have a really bad headache when he wakes, for which they will give him some aspirin, but that's about it.

'He might have dizzy spells or blurred vision too, but again it's a question of staying in bed for a while. Were you thinking of something else?'

'As a matter of fact, yes, I was. I was thinking that he was found on our doorstep and if he just needs some sleep, he might as well stay here. There's no need to drag him off to the hospital and he appears to be a gentleman, so I don't suppose he'll cause any trouble when he wakes up.

'We have a spare bedroom and besides, it seems the Christian thing to do. If there's a problem, we can call you, as you're only two streets away. If he feels all right when he wakes up he can simply be off on his way. What do you think?'

The doctor considered.

'I think it's very kind of you to offer this to a stranger, but if you don't mind taking the Good Samaritan as your model, then I don't see why not. In fact, if he woke up just after they put him to bed in the hospital, it would be a lot of fuss and form filling for nothing.'

'Good, then that's what we'll do. How long do you suppose he might sleep?'

'Well, I really don't know. He could wake at any minute or remain unconscious for the rest of the day, I have no way to tell. If you are quite sure he can rest here, then I'll give you some aspirin, a tincture of iodine and some bandages.

'The wound on his forehead just needs a gentle rinse to remove any grit and then a little iodine to disinfect it. You don't need to do anything complicated, just cover it lightly with a cold damp cloth for a while.

'Then after half an hour or so later cover it lightly with the bandage to keep it clean and in case it weeps a little.

'Then just wait for him to wake up. Is that all right?'

'Oh, yes,' Margaret said, 'that's simple enough. Perhaps when you've finished your tea, and before you go, you can help us carry him upstairs? Then we'll see you as usual after the church service.'

A few minutes later the two men went back to the parlour, the Reverend taking James's legs and the doctor lifting him by the shoulders.

Margaret and Mrs Hodges went upstairs to make the bed, then the men carefully carried the unconscious man upstairs.

The Reverend turned to the ladies.

'Margaret, would you go and get a spare pair of my pyjamas, please? Ian and I will clean him up and change his clothes.

Mrs Hodges, perhaps you could bring another bowl of warm water, flannel and a towel, so that we can bathe his face and hands and clean his wounds while we're about it?'

As they were removing his shoes,

Margaret brought a warm pair of pyjamas from the airing cupboard, placing them on the chair beside the bed.

She then hurried downstairs, as she realised time was passing and very soon the Sunday school needed to start.

Those books were still on the ground by the chapel door, too. It was just as well it wasn't raining.

A Waiting Game

Margaret arrived back at the entrance to the chapel to find the door open, the step wet and the books inside. Clearly Mrs Hodges had taken a moment to come and wash the blood from the step before the children arrived.

Sunday school passed in bit of a blur and Margaret's mind kept drifting to the mystery man and wondering who he was. Finally the class was finished, the children had gone home and she hurried back to ask Mrs Hodges what had happened while she was running the school.

'Well, dear, nothing much, he's still asleep as far as I know. I sat with him for a while, then your father took over because I needed to get down here and start cooking lunch.

'We don't want to leave him alone in case he takes a turn for the worse or wakes up and wonders where he is. In any case, Dr Gordon will be back to look at him again when he comes for tea this afternoon. Perhaps you could go and see if your father needs any help?'

Margaret felt this was bit of an anti. climax. She went up to the spare bed-room and tapped on the door gently before pushing it open and creeping in. Her father was sitting in an upright chair next to the bed, browsing through some papers.

'How is he?' she asked softly.

'He's still asleep and hasn't moved,' her father replied in a low voice, 'but he seems peaceful enough. Do you suppose you could sit with him for a while, as I need to go downstairs and edit this ser-mon for the afternoon service?'

'Of course, just give me a few minutes to put my slippers on and find a book to read while I sit here.'

A few minutes later she was back and sitting in the chair her father had just vacated. She put her book down on the bedside table and studied the man. She thought that yes, cleaned and shaved, he'll be rather more than just handsome.

At a guess, he was a few years older than she was, perhaps twenty-five or so. His black glossy hair stuck out above the bandage around his head like a raven's wing.

He was very rugged, very muscular and very, very masculine. And yet at the same time he was somehow helpless and she felt a surprising urge to protect and care for him. She turned the chair slightly so that she was looking away from temptation and picked up her book. It was a new romance novel. She sighed. Perhaps not the most sensible choice in the circumstances.

But by the time Mrs Hodges came to call her for lunch she had composed herself and was demurely reading chapter three.

* * *

During the afternoon service Margaret wasn't really paying attention to the readings or her father's sermon. Her mind kept drifting to the mystery man just as it had during Sunday school. Who was he?

Why was he in their street at night? Had he woken up yet? It was just as well Ian was finding the correct hymn in the book they were sharing, otherwise she would have had no idea what to sing each time the music started.

At the end of the service, the Reverend stood by the chapel door as usual to exchange a few words with each of the congregation as they left the service. Margaret took Ian's arm and they went on ahead to the manse.

'Has our patient woken up yet?' Ian asked.

She shook her head. 'No, not yet, not unless he woke in the last hour. Mrs Hodges is sitting with him in case he wakes up and wonders where he is.' She felt a glimmer of excitement at the prospect of him waking so they could discover his identity.

'Hmm, yes, that's wise. If he wakes up in a strange place it would be very confusing for him.'

He opened the front door and stood to the side to let Margaret enter first.

'I'll go up now and take a look at him, shall I? I know the way.'

He entered the spare room to find his patient still asleep and Mrs Hodges dozing off in the chair next to the bed. He cleared his throat and she woke up with a start.

'Oh, dear me. Excuse me, doctor, I think I must have been napping.'

'That's quite all right, Mrs Hodges. If our patient had woken up I'm sure you would have woken as well. If you will excuse me now, I'll take a look at him.'

A little later the doctor came downstairs to where Mrs Hodges and Margaret were laying the table for tea. The Reverend was lost in thought gazing out at the garden. He turned around when he heard the doctor enter the room.

'Hello, Ian, how's the patient?'

Mrs Hodges and Margaret stopped what they were doing to listen to the reply.

'He's much the same. He seems comfortable enough and there's little to do until he wakes up.'

'When do you think that will be?' Margaret asked.

'Frankly, I've no idea. We'll just have to wait and see. If he's still sleeping on, let us say, Tuesday, there might be a problem, but we'll worry about that when it happens.'

'Tuesday? But that's two days away. Surely he will wake up before then?'

Ian smiled reassuringly.

'Oh yes, I'm sure he will. There are rare cases where people don't wake up, but it's very unusual and I don't think it likely. It's just because this one has had a very hard knock.'

'In the meantime,' the Reverend said, 'I wonder if we should tell the police about what appears to be an assault and robbery?'

'Why not wait until tomorrow? At this point we don't really know what happened or who he is, so there isn't a great deal we can tell them. All being well, he'll be awake by tomorrow and can tell the police himself.'

'Yes,' the Reverend said, nodding, 'I think you're right, and that way we can leave the police in peace on a Sunday.'

Awake at Last

Margaret awoke early the next morning and hurried to get dressed. After a quick cup of tea and piece of toast in the kitchen, she went back upstairs to see the patient. He was still sleeping quietly.

She put a gentle hand on his forehead. There was a big bump and he felt much warmer than she had expected.

Warm, but not really hot and Margaret hoped it was a reflection of the warm weather rather than a fever starting.

Mrs Hodges had left a bowl of water and some cloths on the chest of drawers. Margaret dampened a cloth and placed it gently on his forehead. She sat in the chair next to the bed and opened her book at the marked place.

After 20 minutes or so, she felt the cloth and realised that it was getting dry. She quietly replaced the cloth but then went to stand looking out of the window.

The cool cloth on his forehead was

enough to wake James.

He came awake very slowly and his eyes fluttered open, only to close again as the light seemed very bright. He also had a splitting headache.

As he came fully awake, he opened his eyes carefully and slowly looked around the room. James didn't recognise it and he had absolutely no idea where he was.

He turned his head slightly to the window where he could see cream curtains waving gently in a slight breeze from the open window.

There was a woman standing there, looking out. She was tall and nicely curvaceous with shining hair that seemed to have a golden halo from the sunlight streaming through the window.

He couldn't quite see her face, but he was certain he didn't know who she was.

James moved to sit up but a pain in his head made him lie back into the pillow, wince and squeeze his eyes shut again.

'You're awake at last!'

He squinted at her but he definitely didn't recognise her.

Even though he had a blinding headache, he still noticed that she looked very happy and was quite beautiful.

The back of his mind made a little note that he would like to get to know her, just as soon as his headache was gone.

'Where am I? And who are you?' A pain stabbed his head as he moved. 'Oh . . . I have a terrible headache.'

'In that case, before anything else, let me give you some aspirin for your headache.'

She put two tablets into a glass on the chest of drawers and added some water from the jug beside it, stirring with a spoon to help the tablets dissolve while she explained.

'You are in the manse, next door to the chapel where we found you unconscious yesterday morning. Here you are, drink this down,' she said firmly, handing him the glass.

He lifted himself carefully on to an elbow, drank the milky fluid down and handed the glass back to her. He slowly and carefully sank back into the pillows and looked up at her.

'What on was I doing in a chapel?'

'Well, you weren't actually in the chapel, I found you on the ground unconscious just outside yesterday morning. We have been wondering who you are and looked for something to find your identity and let your family know, but your wallet was gone and your card case was empty.

'We think you were robbed. It means that we couldn't find out who you were or where you might have come from, so we simply decided to wait for you to wake up.'

He held a hand up to stop her talking.

He liked the sound of her voice but his head was agonising and she was telling him too much, too quickly.

He needed to unde#rstand things piece by piece.

'Wait, wait, just a moment, one thing at a time, please. It's hard to think straight when your head is splitting. You say you found me unconscious outside a chapel?'

'Yes, I was taking books back . . . ' She

stopped as he raised a finger.

'What chapel?'

'The one next door.'

'The one next door. Yes, yes. But where are we?' he said in a slightly tetchy voice.

'We are in . . . Oh, I see your point. You must think I'm a dope,' Margaret said. 'Next door is the Methodist chapel in Elm Road, Ipswich.'

'Ipswich? What the devil am I doing in Ipswich?'

Margaret shrugged.

'And you say you found me unconscious?'

She nodded.

'Yes, in a pool of blood. I thought you were dead at first.'

'Blood?'

'We think somebody hit you on the head and then you fell on the step as well. You had some nasty cuts on your head.'

She pointed at his forehead. James reached up to feel his bandage and winced. It was very sore and he realised he had a large lump under the bandage.

'And this was yesterday? So I've been asleep a whole day?'

Margaret nodded.

'Yes. Just so.'

'And where am I now? I mean, in whose house am I?' he clarified.

'You're in our spare bedroom. In the manse. Next to the chapel.'

'The manse?'

'Oh, it's what they call the house that a Methodist minister lives in. It's next door to the chapel.'

James considered what he had been just told.

'Found unconscious in a pool of blood outside a chapel in Ipswich. And you think I was robbed?'

'Yes, as I said, we looked in your pockets to see who you were but there was nothing to tell us. Don't worry, I'm sure you'll soon remember what you were doing here.

'In the meantime, perhaps you can tell me who you are so we can contact your family?'

He lay back in the bed thinking for

several minutes while Margaret waited for his reply.

'I'm sorry, and you will think this stupid, but I have no idea.' He felt adrift,somehow, and lost.

Margaret stood up straighter and her eyebrows rose in surprise.

'You mean you don't know who you are?'

'No, I really don't. I'm sorry. It's a blank. I can't even think of my own name.'

She sat on the edge of the bed, taking one of his hands in both of hers again and smiled warmly.

'Don't worry, I'm sure it will all come back to you shortly. You've had some nasty bangs on the head. It's not surprising if your head hurts and you can't think clearly.'

He didn't know who he was, why he was here or even where he was. He looked at their clasped hands that were his only anchor in an unknown ocean. She followed his gaze.

She looked back up at him and smiled

back rather tremulously.

Then her eyes widened, she abruptly let go, sprang to her feet and stepped back a little.

He felt the loss.

'You'll feel better when you've rested some more. In the meantime, would you like something to eat?'

He screwed his eyes shut and put a hand to his forehead.

'I hope that aspirin starts working soon, but yes, please, headache or not, I'm starving! And some tea or coffee would be wonderful.'

Margaret left the room and went-downstairs to the kitchen.

'He's awake!'

'Oh, jolly good,' the housekeeper replied, 'I was starting to worry about how long he was sleeping.

'I expect he must be hungry. Get the tray and put some butter and a pot of jam on it. He can have some of this tea and a bit of toast. Then I'll make a proper breakfast for him.

'So, tell me, who is he?'

'That's the strangest thing,' Margaret said slowly, 'he doesn't know. He can't remember.'

A Twinge of Jealousy

The housekeeper stopped what she was doing and turned to look at Margaret in astonishment.

'Good heavens! The man has lost his memory?'

'Yes,' Margaret said, 'but I expect it will all come back to him soon enough.'

Margaret took the tray and went back upstairs, putting the tray on top of the chest of drawers.

She looked at their guest and saw he would have to sit up in order to eat breakfast.

'Just a moment,' she said, taking a spare pillow from the chest. 'Let me put this behind you so that you can sit up better. Now, hold my elbow while I hold yours to pull you up.'

'You mean as if we were going to turn each other in a Scottish reel?'

'Yes, exactly,' she said, grinning, 'but without the music!'

She held his arm as she leaned back and pulled him upright, so as to slip the extra pillow behind his back.

She couldn't help noticing the muscles in his arm and her nerves, already on edge, were set jangling even more than before.

Margaret took a slow calming breath as she turned to get the tray.

'This will get you started, and Mrs Hodges will be along in a moment with something hot.'

'Thank you,' he said. 'Perhaps while I'm eating this you can tell me again who you are. With a bit of luck you will jog my memory.'

'I am Margaret Preston and Mrs Hodges is our housekeeper.'

He looked at her between sips of tea.

'I think you might have said before, but I was a little confused at the time. Are you Mrs Preston? It seems a little improper for us to be alone together in a bedroom.'

'Oh no, I'm Miss Preston. Reverend Preston, my father, is the Methodist

Minister. My mother passed away about ten years ago.

'And since we have the door open, either my father or Mrs Hodges could walk in at any time.'

'Miss Preston! I do believe you are pulling my leg,' he said grinning at her.

Just then Mrs Hodges appeared at the door with another tray.

'Well! Perhaps not entirely,' he continued with a wry grin.

'Good morning, sir. I have some porridge and scrambled eggs on toast for you,' the housekeeper said.

She added the food to his tray.

'Good morning, Mrs Hodges, I presume? I am rather embarrassed at the burden I am imposing on you all.'

'Oh, don't you worry, sir, we're only doing what is right and proper for a Christian household. Now you eat it all up, I'm sure it will help your head.

'I'll ask the Reverend to come and see you shortly and the two of you can discuss what is to be done. Miss Preston can bring the tray down when you have done with it.'

'Thank you, Mrs Hodges,' James said as she left the room.

He turned back to Margaret.

'I hope you don't mind if I get on with my breakfast, and I wonder what else you can tell me to jog my memory.'

'Yes, yes, do. Don't let it get cold.' Margaret sat down in the bedside chair again. 'I'm not sure what else I can tell you. Your clothes were a bit grubby from when you were lying on the ground but Mrs Hodges will have them clean for you soon. There was nothing in your pockets except a handkerchief embroidered with a J.'

'Nothing?'

'No, even your cuff links and hat were gone. Your collar studs were still there, probably because they were under your tie and difficult to remove. Whoever robbed you was very thorough.'

'They must have taken their time, too.'

James finished his breakfast and leaned back on the pillows.

'So, in summary, I don't remember a

thing, and there's nothing to give us a clue except my name starts with a J.'

'I'm afraid that does seem to be the case, plus you get your clothes and shoes made in London,' Margaret said, standing and taking the tray from him.

Her father then came in, having been alerted by Mrs Hodges, and introduced himself.

'I must say it's bit of a setback you not knowing who you are,' the Reverend said. 'It's not a problem for us, but we'll have to change our plan from simply waving goodbye to you, won't we?'

'I feel a bit embarrassed imposing on your goodwill and charity, Reverend, although I'm not sure what I can do about it at the moment.'

'Oh, don't worry, about that, it's no burden and we're quite happy to have you as a guest for a few days, aren't we, Margaret?'

Margaret smiled her agreement at her father.

'We were going to tell the police about you today,' he said, 'but now you are awake we might as well wait a bit longer. I expect your memory will come back shortly. In the meantime, what shall we call you since none of us knows what your name is?'

'It appears that my name starts with a J, so how about John until we know better?'

'Yes, that's a good idea, we do have to call you something,' the Reverend said. 'Now if Margaret would take that tray downstairs, I'll find you a razor. I trust that is safe for you to shave and you don't have double vision? It really wouldn't do to cut your throat at this point!'

James started to laugh, then stopped suddenly and winced, putting a hand to his head. The Reverend waited a moment until Margaret had left the room.

'Now the ladies have left and before you shave, I am guessing you might have other needs since you've been here more than a day. Would you like a chamber pot or shall I help you to the bathroom?'

★ ★ ★

Shortly before lunch the front door knocker sounded and Mrs Hodges opened it to find Dr Gordon standing there.

'Good morning, Mrs Hodges, how is the patient today?'

'Well, doctor, he was awake earlier and talking but with a splitting headache. However, there's a surprising twist . . .' She hesitated and the doctor raised an eyebrow.

'Which is?'

'He says he's lost his memory,' she breathed in a conspiratorial manner. 'He seems polite enough and speaks in a very educated way, but I thought that sort of thing only happened in stories, so can it be true?'

'Don't worry,' the doctor said, 'it does happen sometimes. Not very often, but considering the knocks he has had, it's entirely possible.'

'Well, you've put my mind at rest, doctor. Let me take you to see him.'

He followed her upstairs to the spare bedroom, where she tapped on the door. There was no reply so she eased the door open and looked through the gap to see James stirring awake.

'Hello, sir,' she said, 'the doctor is here to see you.' She opened the door fully for the doctor to enter before pulling it closed behind him.

'Good morning. I'm Dr Gordon,' Ian said, taking the chair next to the bed. 'You've had a nasty bump on the head. How are you feeling?'

'I've still got a thumping headache even after some aspirin and a nap. Also, I seem to have lost my memory. It won't be permanent, will it?'

'No, but you've had a big knock, so your head needs to rest before it all starts working properly again. Sit forward a little please, so I can remove your bandage and take a look at your wounds.'

After checking James's wounds and re-bandaging his head, Ian left the room and went downstairs.

A few minutes later Mrs Hodges looked in to see that James was awake and sitting up.

'Hello, sir. The doctor said to give you

some more aspirin.'

She handed the glass to James.

'Thank you. The doctor said there was no charge for his services because he was a friend of the family,' James said with a raised eyebrow.

'Yes, in a manner of speaking. He and Miss Preston have been stepping out together for quite some time now.'

Mrs Hodges left the room and James settled back down into the pillow and closed his eyes. So the young doctor and the beautiful Miss Preston were a couple, were they?

He felt a slight twinge of regret, or was it sadness, or jealousy? It would be hard to resent the doctor who was Miss Margaret's young man when James was being treated free of charge as a consequence.

Searching for Clues

Margaret was eating breakfast the following day when her father came in to join her.

'John has breakfasted in his room and is feeling better today, but as he's still a little unsteady on his feet, I've put a chair in the bathroom. That way he can wash and shave by himself without danger of falling over with a razor in his hand.

'I just asked Mrs Hodges to put his clean clothes out and when he's ready, and the doctor has seen him, I'll help him downstairs to sit in the drawing-room.'

After the doctor had checked him and said he might go downstairs, James got dressed carefully. He looked around for the bell cord to call a servant to help him.

Servant? Bell cord? What was he thinking? There were no bell cords here and no servants except Mrs Hodges. He didn't know who he was but clearly he was in the habit of calling servants. The

Prestons had said he was expensively tailored and so that fitted.

It was like a jigsaw puzzle where he only had a few pieces and no picture on the box. At least these two pieces seemed to fit together. He gingerly rose to his feet and cautiously made his way to the door. He stopped and held tightly to the door frame. He was feeling dizzy but if he kept himself steady holding the door frame, it would no doubt pass.

* * *

'Reverend,' Mrs Hodges said from the doorway of the drawing-room, 'didn't you say you had a meeting this morning?' She glanced meaningfully at the clock on the mantelpiece.

'Goodness me! You're quite right, Mrs Hodges. Preoccupied with our visitor, I had forgotten about it. Thank you.' He hesitated a moment. 'Margaret, do you suppose you could listen for John and steady him on the stairs? He'll probably be fine but it wouldn't do for him to slip and fall, would it?'

'Of course not, Father, you go to your meeting.'

After her father left, Margaret could hear their guest moving about. She went upstairs to find him standing in the bedroom doorway and holding the door frame.

'Just a moment and I'll help steady you as you go down the stairs.' She hurried towards him.

'Thank you. I felt fine until I stood and moved to the door, then I felt a little dizzy.' He looked at Margaret a bit sheepishly. 'I'm sorry to be such a burden.'

'Nonsense! You've had a hard knock. It's not surprising you feel a bit woozy. Now put your arm across my shoulders and I'll steady you as we go downstairs.'

She put his arm across her shoulders and gripped his wrist in her hand. Then she put her other arm around his waist while he kept hold of the door frame.

She noticed how tall he was, as her face was only just above his shoulder.

He didn't move and Margaret looked up at his face, thinking that perhaps he felt dizzy again.

Instead she found a pair of blue eyes very close to hers and studying her face carefully. Her breath caught and she felt hypnotised.

She just couldn't look away and she felt as if she was the one unsteady on her feet. Without thinking, she pulled him a little closer to steady herself.

They were frozen to the spot for a few long moments and then the sound of Mrs Hodges walking along the hall at the foot of the stairs broke the spell. James cleared his throat and let go of the door frame.

'Perhaps we should try the stairs?'

Margaret was mortified. Here she was, holding his body to hers tightly and staring up into his eyes at a distance of little more than two noses. What must he be thinking of her? She dragged her eyes away and looked down the hallway.

'Yes, we must look where we are going.' As she started moving slowly with James towards the top of the stairs, she wondered exactly where indeed she was going.

At the foot of the stairs Margaret and James released each other cautiously and somewhat self-consciously. James went slowly into the parlour where he sat in an armchair.

As he rested there, with faint household noises in the background, he thought back to the way they had come downstairs. He rather liked the way she pulled him to her side. It was almost an embrace.

He was acutely conscious of how she was a very feminine woman. Then, when she had put her arm around him, he had looked down at her. After a short pause, she had glanced up and then he had found himself looking into Margaret's mesmerising eyes.

Her eyes were wide open and a dark chocolate colour. Like dark pools deep in the forest into which a man could fall and drown happily, James thought to himself and he felt his heart beat faster.

Margaret interrupted his train of thought as she came back in with a tea tray. She put it on the coffee table before taking the other armchair.

'How do you take your tea?' she asked as she poured a dash of milk into each cup.

James stared into space for a long uneasy moment.

'This is ridiculous. I don't even know how I like my tea.'

Margaret thought about it for a moment.

'This morning we gave it to you with no sugar,' she said, 'probably because we didn't think of it, as none of us takes sugar. You didn't object, so let's suppose that's the way you take it too.'

She poured the tea.

James shrugged.

'If only the rest of it were so simple.' He sighed. 'What do you do with yourself when you're not forcing unsweetened tea on an invalid?' he asked, with a carefully straight face.

Margaret looked up, startled, then

relaxed and a glimmer of a smile appeared on her face.

'Not a great deal, really. I run the Sunday school, I help with the housework and the shopping or I run errands now and again for my father.

'If there is nothing else to do, I wait untildark, then I go out with a cosh and find a man whose head wound I can nurse the next day.'

'It must be tricky finding the right man,' James replied in a flat voice. 'Too old and you might kill them. Too young or too married and their family will come looking for them before you have a chance to nurse them.'

'That's true, it's always hard to find the right man,' Margaret said, putting a finger on her chin and frowning, pretending to be thoughtful, 'and in your case I had to stand on a chair to reach high enough.'

They both laughed at the absurdity of the idea but then stopped a little abruptly. Was he married with a wife who was wondering where he was?

After lunch, Mrs Hodges and the Reverend busied themselves elsewhere while Margaret kept James company again in the parlour.

This time Margaret got busy with some darning while James started on a novel from the bookcase. After a while, James's eyelids drooped and he fell asleep in the armchair.

The slight sound of the book slipping from his fingers made Margaret stop her mending and look up in alarm. She studied him carefully for a few minutes to make sure it was just a nap, not something more serious, but when she could see he was breathing deeply, she relaxed again and continued her darning.

I wonder, she thought, is this what life would be like if I married? I would have lunch with my husband and then he would have a nap while I did some mending.

This does rather assume that my husband wouldn't spend all day in an office, but have some less regulated occupation like a minister of religion, or a farmer or even a doctor?

Would this be too dull and unadventurous? No, I don't think so, she decided. There is much to say for contentment and in any case, I wouldn't marry if I didn't love my husband.

She studied James as he slept; he was certainly a good-looking chap and once they got rid of his bandage he would be even more so.

Surely, she thought, there must be a lucky lady somewhere wondering where he had got to? Some rich, pretty young lady with a posh accent, certainly not a very ordinary daughter of a preacher that darns socks.

She shook her head at her train of thought and then bent her head again to the mending.

That evening, the Preston household sat in the parlour a little uneasily as they all wondered what to do now they had a guest.

'Shall we play cards? There are four of

us and we could play Auction Bridge,' the Reverend suggested. 'That is, if you know and remember how to play it, John.'

James searched his memory for a few moments.

'I believe I do and you can remind me, anyway. However, I thought Methodists didn't play cards or drink alcohol?'

'You are correct about the alcohol but we do play cards. Not for money, you understand, because we frown upon gambling.

'However, playing cards only for points or for the sake of winning can be viewed as intellectual sport, rather like chess, so that is not a problem.

'Gambling for money and drinking alcohol can be addictive and a slippery slope down to poverty and destitution. It's a slope we try to help people up rather than let them slide down. So, yes, we do play cards but only as a light-hearted game.'

'In that case, yes I would love to,' James replied.

No News

Lady Radfield was sitting fidgeting in the drawing-room of Westwood Hall after lunch. Her disabled husband, Baron Radfield, was dozing in his wheelchair on the other side of the fireplace.

'George?' she said, looking at her husband who didn't move in response. 'George!' she said more loudly and he sat up blinking sleepily at her.

'George, when did James say he would be back?'

'James? I don't know, I'm not sure if he said. Why? Did you need him for something?' The Baron sounded grumpy after being woken from his nap.

'No, no, I don't particularly need him for anything, but I expected him back on Sunday. It's Tuesday now and we haven't heard from him. He always tells me if he's going to be late home and I'm worried that something has happened to him.'

George was now wide awake and frowning in thought.

'He said he was going to a reunion with some of his army friends, didn't he? Well, he's probably gone off with one of them for a few days, hunting or shooting or fishing or something.'

James's parents had assumed that his army friends were officers of a similar wealthy, aristocratic background.

James had glossed over this point when mentioning the reunion, as he knew his parents would be shocked that some of his friends were poor, badly educated farm labourers.

After several years living in muddy trenches facing an enemy that was trying to kill both you and the people around you, James had come to see people from a different point of view and had re-evaluated what was really important to him in life.

'That's all very well,' Lady Radfield said, 'but why hasn't he let us know?'

'He probably wrote you a note, posted it yesterday and you'll get it tomorrow,

Matilda, so stop agitating!' He picked up 'The Times' that was in his lap.

'But why didn't he telephone? What's the point of having the instrument installed if he doesn't call and say if his plans have changed?'

'We have a telephone. Perhaps they don't. Perhaps they went sailing. Ipswich is on the coast, y'know!'

Lady Radfield stood up and strode off, muttering to herself.

Memories and Temptation

James awoke gradually from a restful sleep during which his head had definitely stopped hurting and the bumps were hardly sore.

He slowly opened his eyes and focused on the wallpaper of the room, puzzled at first that he wasn't in his own bedroom.

Realisation of where he was and why he was there flooded back, followed by the sudden understanding that he could now remember his own room at Westwood Hall.

This surprise was followed by the greater surprise that he also had almost all of his memories back. The only bit he couldn't recall was the bit between saying goodbye to his men at the Rose and Crown and waking up here.

He lay there in the comfort of the bed thinking it all through, remembering waking up and seeing Margaret standing at the window with a halo of light shining around her head like an angel. A guardian angel, perhaps? Angel or not, he felt a great affection towards her and suspected that he was falling in love.

Reality then crashed down on him. Firstly, he remembered he had a fiancée, Anne, and a mother, both of whom were waiting for him to name a wedding date. He had been dragging his feet and now he understood why.

He didn't love Anne, because if he did, he couldn't feel so much more for Margaret, could he?

He and Anne had become engaged during the war while he was on leave but had they really been in love? Now that he could recognise love, he knew he never truly felt it for Anne. Now he was trapped.

He couldn't cry off after all this time and especially when so many men had gone to war and not returned. It would be cruel if Anne never found someone else to marry.

There were thousands of young men lost in the war. Now there were not enough for the all the girls of a similar age hoping to find a husband.

He sighed over the inevitable. He liked Anne even if he didn't love her and they could have a comfortable marriage, even if it couldn't be a love match on his side. He had to carry on with the engagement, not hurt his friend Anne, and do his duty towards her. Even if he loved someone else.

Besides, he thought, Margaret might not feel the same about him and the idea that they could have a shared future was purespeculation. For all he knew she was planning to marry the doctor and was just kind and caring towards him because that was her nature.

That brought him to the second point which he had just realised. If he had regained his memories, there was no reason to stay here.

The idea that he should be on his way home today was unexpectedly depressing. On the other hand, nobody knew that his memory was back. Was it so bad if he failed to mention that happy event for one or two days more?

Life would go on just as normal at home without him to supervise the estate. After all, they had managed pretty well without him while he was away fighting at the front, so they could manage perfectly well without him for another couple of days.

His parents might wonder where he was, but they would probably assume he was staying with some fellow officers for a few extra days.

It was plausible, and it wasn't as if there was any fighting these days, meaning he might not return, was it? Apart from being knocked on the head by a ruffian, he said to himself ruefully.

There was the extra burden he was putting on the Preston family, but they seemed to be comfortably set up and taking it in their stride.

Temptation won.

So, he reflected, staring at the ceiling, that's decided. I'm going to not remember anything for another day. James confessed to himself that he was longing for Margaret's company too, before they were parted for ever.

Then he gave in to temptation completely and decided he might as well be hung for a sheep as for a lamb. He would recover his memory in two days' time, on Saturday, and no sooner.

Still No Word

Thursday came and there was still no word from James. As soon as the postman had called, Lady Radfield went to the stables office to find her younger son.

Roger was busy working at his desk but as his mother came into the room he put down his pen and rose to his feet.

'Roger,' she said, pacing to and fro in front of the desk. 'I am getting worried about your brother. I expected him back on Sunday. It is now Thursday morning, he hasn't returned and we haven't heard a thing. It's not like him.

'Even if he changed his plans, he would surely have found a place from which to telephone and let us know what he is doing, or at least write a note.'

Roger frowned. He hadn't really thought much about what his brother had been doing recently. However, their mother was clearly agitated and he needed to pay attention.

'Yes, Mother, I quite agree, but do we know what his plans were? Or where he went? He said to me he was going to Ipswich, but I didn't ask for any details.' Lady Radfield paused in her pacing and turned to face him.

'No, only that it was to a reunion with men from his regiment somewhere in Ipswich. I didn't see a need to ask more, either. I've looked in his room to see if there was a letter about it, but I found nothing.'

Roger rubbed his chin as he thought about it.

'If there was a letter, he probably took it with him for the address. If we haven't heard from him by tomorrow morning, I'll go over to Bury St Edmunds and see if anyone at the regiment knows about it.'

His mother took a few steps towards the door, then turned to face him again.

'Now we've gone to all the trouble of having the telephone installed, why do we not just telephone them? The army would surely have a telephone, wouldn't they?'

Roger blinked, wondering why he hadn't realised that. The new telephone was going to take some getting used to.

'Yes, of course. I'll do it now.'

A quarter of an hour later, he went into the drawing-room to find his mother in an armchair near the fireplace, crumpling a handkerchief, staring into the distance and looking worried.

His father was sitting in his wheelchair, engrossed as always in his daily newspaper, and clearly didn't want to show any sign of being worried. However, Roger was sure he would be listening carefully to all that went on around him. His mother looked up as he entered the room and he took the chair opposite.

'The Regimental Office says that there was a reunion at the Rose and Crown in Ipswich on Saturday. I spoke to a sergeant who was actually there and he said everything seemed perfectly normal.

'James was there, he seemed in good spirits and nothing seemed to be amiss.

When the sergeant left to get the last train, he thought there were still a few men left talking to James. He couldn't remember exactly who they were, because he had no reason to take note.'

His father lowered the newspaper to look over the top and his mother jumped to her feet. She started pacing up and down the carpet again.

'That doesn't really tell us anything useful, does it? Did he know where James was staying?'

'Yes, apparently James said he was staying at the Lion Hotel because the last train only goes as far as Bury. He was going to walk down to the hotel and get a train in the morning.

'The sergeant was going to catch the train back to Bury St Edmunds as the barracks is only a short walk from the station. And, I agree, it just tells us nothing was wrong on Saturday night and that he was indeed actually planning to return on Sunday.'

Roger paused for a moment in thought.

'Of course, he could have received an

invitation after the sergeant left, but is that likely?'

Lady Radfield stopped in front of the bay window, and stared out at the gardens beyond.

'Who knows? I don't think so. Besides, what about Anne? He knew she was coming this evening and James would never be so rude as to not turn up. Something must have happened to him. Anne will be here this evening expecting to see him. What shall we say?'

She turned back into the room to face her husband and Roger.

'Well,' Roger said slowly, 'we shall just have to tell his fiancée that he's late back. What else can we say? If he doesn't appear by the eight o'clock train this evening I shall have to go to Ipswich tomorrow and ask at the Lion Hotel or the Rose and Crown and see if they know anything.'

'Oh, this is all so perfectly dreadful,' Lady Radfield said, turning back to the window, 'I don't know what she'll think if he's so careless about her.'

'The sergeant did comment that a couple of the men at the reunion lived out this way and he gave me their addresses. One is at Horningsheath and the other at Cheveley. I thought to run over there now and make enquiries.'

His mother sagged with relief.

'Of course. That must be it. He's probably with the Marquess of Bristol at Ixworth or he's called in to the Cheveley Park Stud. Why didn't you say so before? You can bring him back with you and he'll be here before Anne arrives.'

Roger didn't want to contradict his mother, but he thought that both cases were most unlikely because they weren't the addresses he had been given. The sergeant had said that Private Benson lived at one address and Corporal Green at the other.

That James would be at either address seemed improbable, and the only reason for Roger visiting them would be to see if the soldiers had any idea where James had gone.

That these men were not commissioned

officers had been a surprise to Roger. He too had supposed the reunion had been with fellow officers. His brother had been acting a little strangely since he had left the army and Roger was wondering what, exactly, was going on.

Were these other ranks acting as waiters and serving drinks? Probably not, when the reunion was in a public house rather than a hotel or a private house.

He didn't think his mother had noticed that the reunion was at the Rose and Crown. This was rather obviously not a plausible venue for a dinner meeting with officers from the upper class. Perhaps she supposed it was a large inn or a hotel of some sort.

★ ★ ★

It didn't take Roger long to get to Horningsheath where he knocked on the door of Corporal Green's house.

Green's mother directed him to Ickworth House where Green was working as a gardener, but the ex-corporal couldn't help him and so Roger headed on to Cheveley.

The address took him to the middle house of a row of five. This time, the door was opened by a scruffy young man whose left sleeve was empty and tucked into his shirt.

'Private Benson?'

The man stiffened and his eyes narrowed. 'It's just Joe Benson these days.'

'I'm Roger Radfield. You know my brother as Major Radfield.'

Joe's eyes flicked up and down, assessing Roger.

'Yes, I knew Major Radfield. What of it?'

'He's gone missing and I'm trying to find out where he might be.'

'Missing, you say?' Joe paused thoughtfully. 'Won't you come in and take a cup of tea?' he said, taking a step back and opening the door wide.

'Thank you, I will, I'm dry as a bone and the roads are very dusty.'

'Mum!' he called towards the back of the house.'Put the kettle on, will you?

We've got a visitor.' He turned back to Roger and opened a door to the side. 'Take a seat in the parlour, if you please, and tell me how I can help you.'

They went in and sat in two upright chairs, facing each other.

'You went to a reunion in Ipswich on Saturday last?'

Joe nodded.

'I did, sir, and saw your brother and my other old comrades again.'

'I'll get straight to the point, Mr Benson. My brother hasn't returned home yet and I'm trying to find out why not. We expected him back on Sunday and we haven't heard from him. Were you there when he left?'

Joe pursed his lips in thought before replying slowly.

'No. I left nearly at the end and went to stay overnight with a mate in Ipswich. When we left there were a few others still there, including Major Radfield.'

Roger pressed his lips together in frustration at another dead end as Joe's mother came in bearing a tray.

'You work in the village, Joe?'

'I did before the war. I used to be a groom at the stud, but now they say I'm not needed any more on account of people not needing many horses these days. That may be so, but they probably didn't want a one armed groom either,' Joe said with bitterness.

He stood and took a visiting card from the sideboard.

'The major said to contact him if any of us needed work.'

He put the card in front of Roger, who could see it was James's visiting card.

'He said he didn't want to see any of his men without work and I was going to borrow a mate's bicycle on Saturday to go and see the major. There might not be any point if he's not back home yet.'

Roger sat back in his chair as he considered it all.

'If you were a groom, why didn't you join the cavalry?'

'I would've, but the recruiting sergeant said everyone wanted to join the cavalry and they had enough men. He made me join the Suffolks, damn him. Begging your pardon, but it's the way I feel. I wonder if I might still have two arms and a job if I'd joined the cavalry.'

'You still want to work with horses?'

'Oh, I do, and there ain't much I wouldn't need two arms for.'

'I tell you what,' Roger said, who was feeling sorry for Joe, 'I'm going to Westwood Hall now. You get your things while I finish my tea. If my stable master says you know what you're doing, I'll give you a job at the stud.'

Joe's eyes lit up.

'Thank you, sir. I'll really do my best for you. You can't imagine how depressing it is to sit around doing nothing while your parents feed and clothe you.'

*　*　*

It wasn't far to Dullingham and Roger was back in time for lunch. He left Joe in the hands of his stable master. His mother fretted impatiently until the maid had served the soup and left.

'I see you haven't brought James back with you. Did anyone say where he was?' Lady Radfield asked.

'No. Nobody at Ickworth House had any idea where he might be and they didn't know at Cheveley either, so I'm afraid we're no further forward.'

Roger didn't see any need to clarify who he had been talking to. Explaining would only raise questions that Roger neither wanted nor could answer.

'This is terribly annoying. What are we to do next? What shall I say to Anne?' Lady Radfield asked, leaving her soup to go cold.

'I shall have to go to Ipswich tomorrow and make enquiries there. As for Anne, you'll have to tell her the truth.'

Lady Radfield stirred her soup absent-mindedly, still without tasting it.

'She's going to be distressed, coming here to see James and he hasn't even come home.'

Roger was of the firm opinion that Anne might wonder what had happened to James, but she would not get too agitated.

He thought that she was too sensible to turn into a watering pot simply because James wasn't here. Besides, he wasn't convinced that her feelings were that deeply engaged with James, nor his with hers, for that matter.

'If I have to go to Ipswich tomorrow, perhaps it would be best if Anne came with me, otherwise she'll only fidget and get distressed.'

'I don't think that would be appropriate and it's quite likely James will turn up on the afternoon train.'

Guilty Secret

The Preston household ran on tea so the Prestons, Mrs Hodges and James were having a mid-afternoon cup of tea and biscuits together.

'John,' the Reverend said, 'we had intended telling the police about you on Monday in case someone was asking for you, but we never did.

'You seemed to be recovering, so I kept putting it off and now I wonder if there is any point. Do you think we should tell them today?'

James thought about it for a couple of minutes, being careful not to let his gaze drift to Margaret. He was a bit troubled about concealing the return of his memory.

Was he being selfish to want to stay for a couple of extra days? A sort of a holiday before he miraculously recovered? Perhapshe was being ungrateful.

He cleared his throat.

'I must thank you for taking me in as you did and I'm conscious that I'm imposing on your hospitality, so . . .'

The Reverend interrupted him.

'No, no, no . . . don't think of it as an imposition, I wouldn't want you to misunderstand me, you're very welcome and we enjoy your company. I was just worried that someone might be wondering what had happened to you.

'I'm quite happy for you to stay longer but if your memory isn't coming back, then the point must arrive where we start making enquiries.'

James had been about to confess that his memory was almost back and apologise for not saying so before, so was grateful to have been interrupted.

'You are all very kind and I do appreciate it. I'm sure my memory is gradually coming back since I had flashes of returning memories yesterday. I imagine that more memories will return quite soon.' James was rather conscious that more would 'return' just as soon as it was necessary. 'Today is Thursday and fairly late, so why don't we say if I don't know who I am by Saturday morning, we'll call at the police station then?'

The Reverend pursed his lips as he considered the suggestion.

'Yes, that sounds sensible, it's not even another couple of days more, so let's do that.'

Margaret relaxed and sat back in her chair. She hadn't realised until then how tense she had been about the discussion and the prospect of John leaving soon.

She sipped her tea and realised her anxiety was about him leaving, rather than about him not recovering.

It hadn't been clear to her before, but she wanted him to stay and not leave at all which made little sense.

She glanced at James over the rim of her teacup, realising that she had developed some unexpectedly tender feelings for him.

Plan of Action

Thursday afternoon had come and mostly gone by the time Anne's car could be heard on the gravel drive, and there was still no news of James.

Lady Radfield went into the hall as the butler opened the door. Anne handed her hat and gloves to him and came forward to kiss Lady Radfield on the cheek. They went to the conservatory to take tea.

'Anne, I am very embarrassed to tell you that James is not here to greet you. Worse still, we do not know where he is.

'There! I have said the whole dreadful thing all at once when I meant to be more tactful. I'm so sorry, it's because I'm upset about the whole situation.'

Anne looked at Lady Radfield with raised eyebrows and a slightly open mouth for a long moment before recovering from her surprise.

'What has happened?'

'Did you know he was going to an army reunion in Ipswich last Saturday?'

Anne nodded.

'Yes, he did mention it a week or so ago.'

'I expected him back on Sunday but he still hasn't come home. We haven't heard from him and we don't know where he is,' Lady Radfield said as she crumpled her napkin in her trembling hands.

Anne blinked in surprise.

'Are you saying he's disappeared or absconded?'

'I don't know, but something must have happened to him,' Lady Radfield said, dabbing at the corner of her eye with the napkin.

'Perhaps he went off with some friends for a few days.'

'He would have let us know by now by letter or telephone, but there's been nothing.'

'I see. I suppose nobody from the regiment has been in touch?'

'No. Roger called them this morning and then went to see a couple of the other officers that were there, but nobody knew anything.'

Anne moved to put a comforting arm on Lady Radfield's shoulders.

Roger had heard Anne's car on the gravel drive and went to join them. As he arrived, Roger took in the situation of Anne comforting his mother.

'Hello, Anne, I take it Mother has been telling you about James?'

'Yes, she has,' Anne replied. 'It does seem very strange and her ladyship is understandably upset. What do you plan to do next?'

'Mother, I think there is only one thing to be done at this point. Anne and I should go to Ipswich first thing tomorrow morning in the motor car. Then in the afternoon we can start by making enquiries at the Lion Hotel. The weather is warm and if Anne is happy to sit up front in the breeze with me, I'll drive myself and the chauffeur can stay here.'

Lady Radfield frowned at Roger.

'That sounds like a very sensible plan, except that I don't think Anne should go with you. You will have to stay in an hotel for one or even two nights and it isn't proper. You should go on your own and let the chauffeur drive.'

Anne looked from one to the other, but made no comment.

'I understand what you are saying, Mother, but Anne has been betrothed to my brother for nearly four years and she's almost family. Besides, she's probably anxious to help and might feel guilty if she doesn't do something.'

Roger looked to Anne who nodded in agreement.

Silence reigned as Lady Radfield sipped her tea, frowning and deep in thought. She stopped and looked up.

'Perhaps I should go, too?'

'No, Mother, it's unnecessary for all three of us to go and it would be better for you to stay here in case there is a telephone call or some other message.'

'Anne could stay here and I could go with you.'

'Mother, this is your house, not Anne's, and you just can't leave a guest in charge,' he said in a firm tone of voice.

He turned to Anne.

'I beg your pardon, Anne, I don't wish to offend you, but I'm sure you understand.'

Anne waved her fingers dismissively and Roger turned back to his mother.

'We're not likely to meet anyone we know socially in Ipswich and even if we did, they would soon appreciate the special circumstances.'

'Very well,' Lady Radfield said with a sigh. 'I suppose unusual situations call for unusual measures, but I'm not at all happy about it.'

Out of the Blue

There was a knock at the front door in the middle of the afternoon and Mrs Hodges opened it to find Dr Gordon on the step.

'Good afternoon, doctor, do come in. Have you come to see the patient or is it your afternoon off?'

'It's both, really. Is it convenient?' he said, stepping into the hallway.

'Of course it is, doctor. John is in the parlour with the Reverend and Margaret. Shall I ask him to step into the dining-room to see you there or would his bedroom be more appropriate?'

'I'm sure the dining-room will be perfectly adequate, Mrs Hodges. I know my way, so perhaps you will be kind enough to let him know that I'm here?'

The doctor examined John and declared himself satisfied, especially when he was told some memories were returning.

'Well, you are fit to travel, the only

question is where to?' the doctor asked with a wry smile.

James smiled faintly back at the doctor. Come tomorrow this little interlude and charade would be over, although the doctor couldn't know this.

Somehow he hadn't managed to settle back into his former life after leaving the army and this week of nothing to do and no responsibilities had given him a chance to think things through.

Unfortunately, it seemed that he was going to have to marry a fiancée that he no longer loved and leave behind someone that he thought he was coming to love. But at least now his path was clear.

They both rose and returned to the parlour, the doctor leaving his bag on the hall table as they passed through, to find the other three anxiously awaiting his opinion.

'Well, Ian,' the Reverend said, 'what's your verdict? He's certainly looking better and it's reassuring that some memories are coming back, isn't it?'

'Oh, yes, definitely. I was just saying

to John that I'm optimistic he will get his whole memory back very soon, but I emphasised that he just has to be patient and wait for it to happen. In any case he doesn't need to see me again.'

He paused a moment and took a breath before continuing.

'While I am here, Reverend, there is another matter I would like to speak to you about, in private, if I may?'

'Of course. Let's go into my study.'

The doctor and the Reverend left the room and walked down the hall to the study, followed by Mrs Hodges on her way to the kitchen.

Back in the parlour Margaret turned to James.

'This is good news, isn't it? I wonder what you will remember next.'

James smiled as he considered what to say, unable to speak the truth but not wanting to lie to her.

'Who knows?'

The parlour door opened and Mrs Hodges came back in with a tray of tea-cups and saucers, a sugar bowl and milk jug that she put on the table. She then bustled off back to the kitchen for the teapot and a plate of biscuits.

The Reverend Preston entered his study, waited for the doctor to follow him and then closed the door behind them. He sat behind his desk in the study and indicated that the doctor should take the seat in front of it.

'Now then, Ian, what was it you wanted to talk about?'

The doctor sat and rested his elbows on the arms of the chair, steepled his fingers together against his lips and gazed at the green leather top of the desk for a few moments while he gathered his thoughts. He lifted his eyes and looked at the Reverend.

'As you know, Margaret and I have been seeing each other for quite a while now and I have developed a great affection for her.'

The Reverend's eyes opened slightly in surprise at the topic.

'And for a couple of months now, I have been a partner in the practice, so

I am well able to support a wife and, eventually, children. I would like your permission to ask Margaret for her hand in marriage.'

The Reverend sat a little straighter in his chair.

'Well, goodness me! I'm very happy to grant the permission and I will be just as happy to welcome you as a son-in-law,' the Reverend said, smiling broadly, 'but I must confess you have caught me by surprise, as I hadn't realised that things had progressed that far!'

'I wasn't really planning to declare myself so soon, but the other day you were all talking about your move to Cambridge and it made me realise that the move was only a few weeks away,' the doctor explained.

'Then I knew that I wanted her to stay here with me and obviously the answer was to ask her to marry me.'

The Reverend paused for a moment to take stock.

'Ah, yes, I see your point. To be honest, I was preoccupied with the church aspects of the move and I suppose I just assumed Margaret and Mrs Hodges would sort out the rest between them.

'I'm afraid I hadn't really considered the consequences for yourself and Margaret. I can see now that I have to give everything else a bit more thought.'

He sat quietly, thinking, for a few moments more while Ian waited patiently, then gave a start.

'Yes, well, I suppose I had better ask Margaret to come and see you,' he said, with raised eyebrows. 'Wait here a moment and I'll go and get her.'

He stood up, came around the desk and shook Ian's hand before opening the door and returning to the parlour and as he entered they looked up.

'Margaret, would you go to the study, please? There is something that Ian wants to speak to you about.'

Margaret was surprised, but left the room without saying anything. James and Mrs Hodges looked at each other and then again at the Reverend, who said nothing but picked up his tea cup and sat in an armchair, lost in thought.

James and Mrs Hodges looked at each other once more with questions in their eyes, but said nothing and continued drinking their tea.

Unexpected Proposal

Margaret entered the study, closed the door behind her and said quietly and somewhat nervously, 'You wanted to speak to me, Ian?'

Ian rose to his feet, went to stand in front of Margaret and took her hands gently in his.

'Yes, Margaret. We've known each other for some time now and I have become very fond of you.'

Margaret's eyes widened at the direction of the conversation and she looked intently at Ian's face.

He continued.

'I've realised that if you move to Cambridge there will be an empty hole in my life without you. I wouldn't want that to happen, so will you do me the honour of becoming my wife?'

Margaret just stood there, her lips slightly open, gazing at Ian in complete surprise. She had had vague thoughts of marriage from time to time but had never really given it any serious thought, nor to marrying Ian.

She realised that her mouth was open, closed it with a snap and dropped her eyes to his chest while she tried to get her jumbled thoughts into order.

Not only had she not thought of getting married any time soon but she was not at all sure she wanted to marry Ian.

She liked him, he was a good friend and they enjoyed each other's company. He would make a good husband but was he the husband for her?

If she said 'No', she might be throwing away a chance of a good marriage, she would probably lose a good friend and would hurt him at the same time.

Saying 'Yes' could equally well be a mistake – was it love they felt between them or just friendly affection? Saying 'Yes' but asking for a long engagement so as to be clear in her mind wasn't an option when they were moving house in a few weeks.

Time passed slowly and he smiled

hesitantly, watching some of the emotions flitting across her face.

She looked up and gave him a little nervous smile in return.

'I don't know what to say. I haven't given any serious thought to marriage.' She looked anxiously at Ian.

'Really, this is unexpected. I need to think, do you mind? Please don't think this is no. Or yes. I'm just flustered!'

'I understand,' Ian said, smiling. 'Your father was caught by surprise, too. How long do you need?'

'Until tomorrow?'

'I'm sure I can manage until tomorrow,' he said. 'In the meantime, remember there's the dance at the Corn Exchange tonight. Shall I come back to collect you at seven o'clock?'

'Yes, yes, seven is fine,' she said rather faintly.

He leaned forward and brushed his lips gently across hers while she stood there in a daze.

'Until seven then,' he said softly. 'I'll let myself out.' He released her hands, opened the study door, collected his black bag from the hall table and left the house.

★ ★ ★

From the parlour Mrs Hodges heard the front door open and close, and she waited for Margaret to return.

After a few moments it was clear that she wasn't going to, so she glanced at the Reverend, who still sat in his armchair deep in thought and then she stood quietly and went to the study.

She looked in at the open door and found Margaret still standing where Ian had left her, gazing into the distance and as deep in thought as her father was.

'Well?' Mrs Hodges said, suspecting but not really sure of the question she was asking.

'He asked me to marry him,' Margaret replied, turning to face her but looking in a rather unfocused way.

'And?' Mrs Hodges prompted, a touch impatiently.

101

'I don't know. I wasn't expecting it. I said I would give him an answer tomorrow.' Her attention snapped back to Mrs Hodges. 'I think I should go to my room now because I need to think a little and also get ready for the dance tonight.'

Mrs Hodges was surprised. Not surprised that Ian had asked Margaret, she had been expecting that for a while. No, she was surprised that Margaret hadn't accepted him immediately.

She stepped back from the study doorway and watched thoughtfully as Margaret came out of the study and slowly went upstairs.

Behind Mrs Hodges, the parlour door opened fully, the Reverend stepped into the hall and looked at Margaret going upstairs and then raised his eyebrows enquiringly at Mrs Hodges.

'She's thinking about it and going to answer him tomorrow,' she said, then paused and studied the Reverend's reaction.

This was clearly not what the Reverend had expected, either, and he could only say 'Oh,' before he frowned slightly, hesitated and then went into the study, deep in thought.

Mrs Hodges watched him with her hands clasped at her waist. As he turned into the study she shook her head slightly in exasperation at both of them and turned the other way towards the kitchen.

While Mrs Hodges had been speaking to Margaret, she had left the parlour door ajar and John could just hear the conversation between the two of them They hadn't said much, but those few words felt like a knife to his heart and he suddenly realised that he was jealous, very jealous.

He wondered why and then realised with a shock that he wasn't merely falling in love with her but that he had already fallen completely in love with Margaret over the last few days.

Frustratingly, he could see that there was nothing he could now say or do. Besides, how could he say or do anything when he supposedly didn't even know who he was?

Worse still, he was duty bound to go home and marry Anne.

Sadness and regret washed through him and he was glad that he had already decided to leave tomorrow and carry on with life as it had been before. There was no other possible or sensible course but to move on and try to forget her.

* * *

Margaret went to her room and sat on the bed in a daze. Ian had asked her to marry him when she really hadn't given any serious thought to marriage. Now she had to consider her future.

Did she love Ian? She certainly liked him. She was very fond of him. But she wasn't at all sure that she loved him. Perhaps love would grow with time. Did he love her? He hadn't said so, but would he ask her to marry him if he didn't?

Her thoughts were in a whirl and she really couldn't think straight. She needed more time to sort her feelings out and understand if they loved each other or not, but this move to Cambridge wasn't going to allow her time. Marriage was for ever and she didn't want to marry without love.

On the other hand, if she didn't marry Ian, would she ever marry? So many men had died in the war that there were a lot more women than there were men to go around.

She might never again meet someone as warm, handsome and with such a good career as Ian. But without love, she didn't think she could do it. If she didn't marry Ian and never met anyone else, she could simply look after her father.

There would be no family of her own and no children, but she would still have the Sunday school and those children to care for, although it could never be the same as having children of her own.

Then it struck her that while she might have accepted Ian's proposal two weeks ago, now she had met John. Suddenly Ian just didn't seem right any more, even if she didn't really know who John was or where he came from.

Had it been John asking, she would probably have said yes anyway, even knowing so little about him. The sensible voice in her head told her that if she didn't love Ian, and she could see now that she definitely didn't, then she had to refuse him.

Tonight would be the last time they went out together, because after she refused him, they couldn't continue, as Ian, at least, needed to find someone else.

As for John, it was clear from his clothes and accent that he was from a wealthy upper class family. It seemed improbable that he would ever consider marrying the middle-class daughter of a Methodist minister, even if, as he had suggested, he wasn't already married.

She had to make some sort of plan for her future, as drifting along as she had been would no longer do.

Acting as housekeeper for her father was a sensible possibility, she thought, because when he moved to Cambridge he would need a new housekeeper and she was old enough now to do that for him.

She must remember to ask Mrs Hodges if she was still planning to go and live with her sister or if she had decided to look for another housekeeping position.

She would be sad to part from Mrs Hodges because they had become very good friends in six years and sometimes she felt like the mother Margaret had lost.

Margaret sighed. They had all been so very comfortable and now, suddenly, everything was going to change for all of them, one way or another.

She looked at her alarm clock on the bedside table. Where had the time gone? It was time to go downstairs and have something to eat before getting dressed.

I Thought You'd Never Ask!

Ian had called for Margaret and they had gone off to the centre of town. John had gone for a short walk. Now was the customary time for Mrs Hodges and the Reverend to sit in the parlour and read for a while before retiring for the night.

Margaret had a key and didn't need them to wait up, and John would be back soon. Mrs Hodges picked up the novel she had started and settled comfortably into an end of the sofa.

The Reverend came into the parlour and, instead of finding his own book, went and sat next to Mrs Hodges. She looked up in surprise. The Reverend usually sat in his favourite armchair, not on the sofa.

'Mrs Hodges,' he said, 'Ian reminded me it's only a few weeks until the move to

Cambridge and he also made me realise I really hadn't given the move enough thought. I've been here nearly six years now and I suppose moving had always seemed a long way off.'

Mrs Hodges' heart sank. She knew that her time as a housekeeper here was nearly at an end, but she'd become very fond of the Reverend and his daughter, so she hadn't wanted to think about it. Seeing them leave was going to be a terrible wrench.

She had an invitation to go and live with her sister, but it would be like retiring, and she wasn't ready mentally or financially to do so.

At the same time, she hadn't found any enthusiasm to seek a new housekeeping post. She felt a wave of sadness wash over her as she realised it was time to face up to it.

The Reverend cleared his throat nervously and she looked up at him, realising it might be difficult for him too.

'Mrs Hodges, we've got to know each other quite well in six years and . . . ' He hesitated before continuing in a rush, 'and it wasn't until Ian was talking about Margaret going and leaving him behind that I realised as well that I couldn't bear to go and leave you behind as well.'

Mrs Hodges' eyes widened and her mouth dropped open. This was not what she had been expecting.

The Reverend took Mrs Hodges' hands in his.

'It's made me understand that some time over those years, I'm not sure when exactly, I've fallen in love with you and can't bear to part from you. I don't know what you might feel for me but, Mrs Hodges – Frances – will you marry me and come with me to Cambridge as my wife?'

After the momentary shock, Mrs Hodges squeezed his hands and tears started to roll down her face.

'Oh yes, Reverend, yes please, I never imagined that you would ask, but nothing would make me happier!'

'In that case, perhaps you would call me Hugh and let me dry your tears?'

'Oh yes, Hugh, you may, but do first kiss me.'
And he did.

Investigations Begin

Roger enjoyed driving the Daimler. Sometimes it was convenient for the chauffeur to drive them somewhere, but it wasn't the same as driving it yourself. It was especially enjoyable when it was a warm sunny day and the passenger seat was occupied by a pretty girl.

He turned his head and looked at Anne appreciatively. She was wearing a tight-fitting pink cap with a red ribbon around it and her blonde hair poked from the bottom edge. She wore a scarlet dress with rows of fringes from top to bottom that fell like a waterfall.

Anne caught him looking at her and smiled.

'What is it?'

'You look like strawberries and cream and good enough to eat!'

She laughed.

'I think you should be watching the road and concentrating on where we are going!'

He did as she said and she studied his profile in turn. He bore a close resemblance to James and it was very easy to guess that they were indeed brothers.

But where James was very tall with jet black hair like his father, Roger was only just over average height and had the same dark brown hair as his mother.

James had bright blue eyes and Roger had dark brown but there the differences ended. Both of them had the same firm jaw and well proportioned features that gave them a classically handsome profile.

Early in the afternoon, Roger and Anne arrived in Ipswich and parked outside the Lion hotel.

'Good afternoon, sir and madam,' the assistant behind the desk greeted them, peering over his spectacles, 'are you staying here tonight?'

'Yes, we have two rooms reserved for Mr Radfield and Miss Harper.'

'Ah, yes, very good, sir, we have been expecting you. Perhaps if you would sign the register while we get your luggage from your car.'

He beckoned a bellboy hovering at the end of the counter and indicated that he should go and get them. He then turned and removed two keys from the hooks behind him and put them on the counter.

'There we are sir, rooms six and seven. Will you be eating in the restaurant this evening?'

Roger turned to Anne who shrugged and nodded. Roger turned back to the desk clerk.

'Yes, a table for two at seven, thank you. Now before we go up to our rooms I need to ask you something. My brother, James Radfield, was due to stay here last weekend. Can you tell me if he did so?'

The clerk looked up sharply.

'Ah! Would you excuse me a moment, sir? I'm sure the manager would like a word with you.' So saying, the clerk tapped on a nearby door before entering and closing it behind himself.

Roger and Anne looked at each other

worriedly as they heard a murmur of voices from the office. Moments afterwards, the door opened again and the clerk emerged.

'If you would be so kind as to step into his office, the hotel manager Mr Robbins would like to speak to you.'

Roger and Anne went around the end of the desk and into the office where the slightly portly hotel manager was standing behind a desk.

'Mr Radfield, I'm very pleased to see you, as we have become concerned about your brother. Please take a seat.'

'Is my brother ill then?' Roger asked in concern as they all sat down.

'No, no, sir, that's not it. He seems to have disappeared and we're not sure what has happened. If I may explain . . .

'He checked in on Saturday and went out that evening, but hasn't been seen since. We would have contacted you, but we found we had insufficient detail to do so.

'The bed hasn't been slept in and although we expected him to be leaving on the Sunday or Monday, he hasn't been seen since the Saturday evening. He ate an early dinner in the restaurant that evening and then went out.

'When he didn't sleep here the Sunday night either, we reported it to the police first thing on Monday morning but they knew nothing.

'They said they would check at the hospital, but we haven't heard anything since then and I'm supposing that the police don't know any more.'

Roger paused thoughtfully as he mulled over the explanation.

'Thank you. That is why we've come to Ipswich, because he hasn't returned home, we haven't heard anything and so we've come to look for him. Do you know what was he wearing when he went out?'

'Well, yes, sir, the porter recalled that he went out wearing a dark lounge suit and a brown Homburg but not carrying a coat because the evening was warm.'

'Definitely not evening wear?'

'That is correct, sir, the porter was

116

quite definite it was a lounge suit, not a tailcoat or dinner jacket.'

'Roger,' Anne said, 'that makes sense if he was going to an informal reunion in a public house. I can't imagine him wearing a tailcoat for something like that, especially if it was, as we think, all ranks and not just officers.'

'Yes, yes, you are quite right, Anne, it's all consistent.'

He looked back to the manager.

'Thank you for your concern and assistance. I think we had better visit the police and then the Rose and Crown to see if we can discover more. Perhaps someone could make a note of the directions and in the meantime we'll go up to our rooms and refresh ourselves.'

'Certainly, sir,' Mr Robbins said, moving around his desk and opening the door for them. 'I'll get the front desk to draw a small map and add the addresses ready for when you come down.'

Quarter of an hour later, Roger and Anne met in the hotel lobby and followed the desk clerk's directions to the nearby police station.

There they met the detective in charge of the case who had no more information to offer them. The police had made extensive enquiries but nobody answering the description had been seen. The police had not been aware of the reunion at the Rose and Crown. Roger gave them his details before leaving.

'What shall we do next?' Anne asked as they stood on the pavement outside.

'The reunion was to take place at the Rose and Crown public house, so let's find it and see the landlord. He might give us a clue, failing which we will have to visit some of the other men that were there and see if they know anything.'

Finding that the Rose and Crown was only a little further up the same road, they continued walking up the street, even though it was still too early for the pub to open for the evening. It was easy to find on the corner of a crossroad. The landlord answered the knock on his door promptly.

'I'm sorry but we're closed until six-thirty, you'll have to come back later.'

'We don't want a drink, we're looking for a missing person and think you might be able to help.'

'A missing person?'

'Yes, my brother came to a reunion in your function room last Saturday but he seems to have disappeared.'

'Oh. I see. You had better come in.' The landlord opened the door wider and invited them to sit around a table in the saloon bar.

'Disappeared, you say?'

'Yes, we know he was there, because somebody saw him, but he never came home. The hotel says he never returned there either, so we don't know where he's gone. We thought he might have gone off with some friends, but that can't be it because he would have said something to the hotel.'

The landlord rubbed his chin thoughtfully.

'I wonder if my wife might have an idea?' He stood and opened a door at the back of the bar. 'Betty! Betty! Come here a moment, I need you.'

A plump lady wearing an apron and drying her hands on a towel came to the door.

'One of the people at that reunion has gone missing. Did you notice anything unusual when you were clearing up?'

'Missing you say? Well I never. Can't say as I noticed anything particular. What did he look like?'

'This is his brother,' Anne said, 'they look very alike except the brother is a bit taller, has black hair and blue eyes.'

The landlady took a good look at Roger. 'Ah, yes, I remember him. Me and Gertie noticed him because he was a good-looking chap. Broad shoulders, I recall. Nice suit, brown stripe, with a Homburg hat. Yes, he came out of the gents just as we started to clear the table. Polite too, he wished us good night as he left.'

'Did anybody else leave with him?' Roger asked.

'No. He was the last one out. We bolted

the door as soon as the table was clear and we'd checked to make sure nothing had been left behind.'

'I see. Did he look well? Not ill or drunk too much?'

The landlady shook her head slowly.

'No, he looked fine, nothing unusual.'

'You have been most helpful,' Roger said, rising to his feet and shaking hands with the landlord and Betty. 'At least we now know he went missing between here and the hotel.'

Roger and Anne left the pub and turned to walk slowly back towards the hotel.

'I have to say I'm a bit disappointed,' Roger said, as Anne took his arm. 'They haven't told us much we didn't already know.'

'Well, that's not quite correct,' Anne replied. 'He said that nothing unusual happened, which suggests that the meeting was orderly. No arguments or fights, for example.'

'True, but I never really considered that likely. I'm sure military discipline would have persisted, even if they were out of uniform, especially with officers there.'

'Now I hesitate to say this,' Anne said, 'but it's been going around my head since yesterday. You don't suppose he's disappeared deliberately, do you?'

Roger stopped in surprise and turned to face Anne.

'Deliberately? What do you mean?'

'Well, as you know, I've been helping out at the hospital for the last few years with the injured soldiers. You would think by now that most of the injuries would have healed and the men gone home. But there are still some men in the hospital with injuries you can't see.

'They've left the army and returned home but then find they can't cope with normal life. In the army it's mostly routine and you are told what to do, so you don't have to make any decisions and you could drift along in a haze. It's a way of coping with the horror and stress of the war.

'When they get home it's not like that.

A few can't cope and they retreat into a kind of protective shell. It's as if they are in a state of shock that doesn't end. They can't shake it off and they sit in the hospital gazing at the wall or the garden.

'We've had a couple of men who simply walked out and disappeared, probably to become the tramps that you sometimes see walking along country roads.'

Roger looked at Anne thoughtfully for a couple of minutes while she studied his face in return.

'No Anne, he's been very quiet since he left the Army but I can't believe he's done that. He's been out of the army for six months now and coping perfectly well with running the estate.

'I know I've been busy running the stud but I'm sure I would have noticed if he was struggling. Have you seen any problems?'

'No,' she replied, 'nothing specific but a bit subdued, as you say. However, meeting the old soldiers could have triggered something. I have to say he's changed in the last two or three years.

'He seems rather more serious these days and given to long, quiet, reflective periods but that's all, I think. It's hardly surprising after four years of war and all the deaths and injuries.

'Your mother has been pressing us to pick a wedding day, but neither of us has been in a hurry to do it. I can't imagine the pressure would be enough to make him run off.' She smiled wistfully. 'It would be rather embarrassing for me if that turns out to be the case, wouldn't it?'

Roger took her right hand in his left and rubbed it gently with his other hand.

'Now, now, you mustn't think things like that, it's inconceivable. You're intelligent, pretty, well connected, charming and generally a wonderful person.

'Nobody would run away rather than marry you, why, if you weren't engaged to my brother I'd marry you myself!' As he said it, it somehow that didn't seem like the strange idea that it should have seemed.

Anne looked into his eyes. She sighed and shook her head gently.

'Roger, you're such a flatterer. Come along, let's go back and have dinner.' So saying, she took his arm again and turned them back the way they had been going to the hotel.

It was still a little early for dinner when they got there, so they continued walking past the hotel into the town centre, idly looking into shop windows as they went by. As they passed the Corn Exchange, Anne suddenly stopped and clutched Roger's arm.

'Oh, just a moment Roger, let me see what it says on that poster.' They took a couple of steps back to look at the poster on the column at the side of the entrance doors.

'I thought so, it's a dance here this evening. Do you suppose we could go? I do so love to dance.' Anne looked at Roger, blatantly doing her best to look wistful and appealing.

Roger just laughed.

'You're a manipulating disgrace!' He paused for a moment's reflection. 'Oh very well, yes, why not? The alternative is to just sit around in the hotel bar and since my charming companion in both cases is the same, going to the dance sounds much more interesting.'

Anne grinned at him and then her face suddenly clouded.

'Oh, Roger, do you think it proper? After all, we are supposed to be looking for James, not indulging in frivolity.'

Roger patted her hand gently.

'There's nothing much we can do this evening, so it doesn't make much difference, does it? Besides . . . ' Roger was about to say, 'Besides, he's just missing, not dead.'

Somehow that didn't seem like a good thing to say right now, especially when he had a niggling worry at the back of his mind that something was seriously wrong. He was not going to frighten Anne by talking about the worst case.

'Besides,' he continued, 'we need to relax, so that we sleep properly and are refreshed to resume the search tomorrow.' He thought that sounded a rather lame thing to say but saw that Anne was no longer concentrating on what he was saying anyway.

'I can't go in any case, I didn't bring a ball gown,' Anne said, frowning and biting her bottom lip.

'Ball gown?' Roger said, raising his eyebrows in amusement. 'My dear, this is a provincial town dance, not a ball at Carlton House!

'The dress you have on would be perfectly suitable for example, and for myself I only brought a lounge suit, nothing more formal, so that will have to do. It starts at seven-thirty, so if you still want to go, we should get back to the hotel now, so as to eat and freshen up in good time.'

The matter settled, they turned and walked back towards the hotel. Roger noticed that she was quiet and looking thoughtful.

'A penny for your thoughts?' he asked, looking at her.

'I think I shall change into a new dress that I just happened to have brought with me,' she said, smiling up at him.

No Good Dreaming

Dinner was over and Roger had been to his room to freshen up and change into his lounge suit. Now he was waiting in one of the armchairs in the hotel lobby.

Light blue silk swaying gently as it came down the stairs caught his eye and he stood and stared.

Anne was wearing a light sleeveless blue silk dress printed with large cream coloured flowers. It had three large flounces below the waist and a cream sash at the waist tied into a large bow on the left hand side.

On her arm was a small beaded bag and her shoes were a matching cream. She reached the bottom of the stairs and gave Roger a dimpled smile.

'Roger,' she whispered as she leaned towards him, 'close your mouth and start breathing!'

Roger shook himself.

'I'm sorry, I was lost there, you look

absolutely stunning.'

'Come along, then,' she said, looking a little smug. 'Stop standing around like a simpleton, take me dancing!'

Roger looked back at her. It probably was a bad idea, but when she looked at him like that she was hard to resist. As soon as they found James, he was going to put her firmly in James's arms, stand well away and let James deal with her. She was an unhealthy temptation.

Anne walked along with smile on her face and a slight spring in her step.

Roger was starting to wonder if bringing Anne to Ipswich and then going dancing alone with her was such a good idea after all.

They bought their tickets and walked into the Corn Exchange to find that the dancing was already underway and the hall was starting to fill up.

'Look,' Roger said, pointing down the left hand side of the hall, 'there's a table there with a smart looking couple and two free chairs. Perhaps they wouldn't mind us joining them.'

They walked around the dance floor and approached Margaret and Ian sitting at the table.

'Excuse me,' Roger said to them, 'do you mind if we join you if these chairs are free?'

'No, not at all, please do,' Ian replied, who rose to his feet and pulled out a chair for Anne.

'Thank you. I'm Roger Radfield and this is my friend, Anne Harper,' Roger said, offering his hand to Ian.

Ian shook his hand and then Anne's hand.

'Pleased to meet you. This is Margaret Preston and I'm Ian Gordon.'

Anne shook Margaret's hand.

'How do you do?' She smiled.

'Very well, thank you,' Margaret replied. 'What a lovely dress you are wearing!'

'Oh, thank you. I was in London last week, saw it in a shop window and couldn't resist.'

As the girls continued chattering, the two men looked at each and grinned.

'Shall we get drinks from the bar while

they discuss fashion?' Ian asked.

'Yes, I think that would be an excellent idea.'

A few minutes later they returned from the bar with a drink in each hand to find the ladies deep in discussion as if they had been friends for years.

'Enough talking,' Anne said, standing and taking Roger's hand, 'we came here to dance and this is a foxtrot which is my favourite.'

Margaret squeezed her lips together so as not to laugh at the little boy expression on Roger's face. Ian and Margaret watched them progressing around the crowded dance floor.

'They are a bit posher than the usual that we meet here,' Ian remarked, 'but they seem nice enough.'

'Yes, they are, and they dance very well,' Margaret replied, still watching them move around the floor. 'He looks vaguely familiar to me, but I can't place him, can you?'

Ian sat up straight so as to see him better, as Roger and Anne moved between other couples on the dance floor.

'No, I can't say I can. And I certainly haven't seen her before either.'

Margaret batted his arm with the back of her hand.

'It's about time you asked me to dance!'

'Yes, dear, whatever you say, dear,' Ian said, grinning at her, 'but this song is nearly ended, so let's wait for the next one to start.'

A moment later the music finished and Roger and Anne walked back to the table from the other side of the floor. Just before they got there the band struck up with a waltz and Ian and Margaret took to the floor.

At the end of that dance, when Ian and Margaret had returned to the table, Anne remarked that the band was very good and the floor was excellent.

'Yes,' Margaret said, 'it's a very good venue and we usually come for the monthly dance. Have you been here before?'

'No, we live near Newmarket and

we're just visiting. It's pure chance that we saw the poster at the entrance as we passed it this afternoon.'

'That's curious, because I was just remarking to Ian that Roger seemed faintly familiar, but I couldn't think why.' She turned to Roger and studied his face for a moment. 'Can you think of a reason we may have met before?'

'No, I'm sorry, I have no idea and I don't even remember the last time I was in Ipswich,' he said, gently shaking his head.

Before they could talk further, the Master of Ceremonies spoke up.

'Ladies and gentlemen, may I have your attention! The next dance is the first of our Ladies' Excuse Mes. I remind the ladies that we expect them to ask a gentleman to dance with whom they have not danced so far this evening.'

The two couples turned back to face each other and Anne immediately offered her hand to Ian.

'May I have this dance, sir?'

'But of course, it will be my pleasure,'

Ian said, standing and leading her on to the dance floor.

'May I?' Margaret asked of Roger, offering her hand.

'I would love to,' he replied, standing and leading her on to the dance floor as well.

'As I was saying,' Roger said to Margaret as they started to move around the floor, 'I can't recall the last time I was in Ipswich and the only reason that we are here now is that my brother has gone missing and we've come to look for him.'

Margaret looked up sharply at Roger's face and suddenly stopped.

'Of course, I see the resemblance now!'

Roger was caught off balance by the sudden stop and had to apologise to a couple that nearly ran into the back of them.

'Come to the side of the floor a moment,' he said, trying to get out of the way of couples coming around the now very crowded dance floor. 'Now, what do you mean, resemblance?'

Margaret was excited now.

'Does your missing brother have black hair, blue eyes, and is a bit taller than you?'

'Yes! Have you seen him somewhere?'

'I have,' she said triumphantly, 'we've got him at home!'

Roger looked down at her in amazement. 'At home? What is he doing at your home?'

'He had a fall and lost his memory. I found him on the chapel steps so we took him in while he recovered. Shall we go and tell the others?'

Roger was totally astonished and just stood there staring at her until she pulled his hand and headed back towards their table. They made their way back just as the music was coming to an end and Ian and Anne came back to join them.

'Ian! Ian! I think we found out who John is – it's Roger's brother!' Margaret cried excitedly as the other two arrived back at the table.

'No, no, there must be a mistake,' Roger said, putting his hands out flat to calm them down. 'My brother's name is James.'

'James? Oh, quite possibly,' Margaret continued excitedly. 'We just call him John because we didn't know his real name and he had a handkerchief in his pocket with a monogrammed J. Now, Ian, look at Roger here and tell me if he looks like John or not? Or do I mean James, now?'

Ian turned and studied Roger for a moment.

'Well, yes, now I stop to think about it, I do see the resemblance. How remarkable!

'Actually I'm his doctor and I confess I was starting to wonder how long it would be before he got his memory back. He has had some bits and pieces come back, but nothing substantial. Hopefully when he sees you and your young lady it will prompt rather more memories to return.'

'I certainly hope so, since Anne is not my young lady so much as his fiancée and it would be rather embarrassing if he couldn't remember either of us.

'In fact, if we try to take him home when he doesn't know us he might think he is being abducted!'

Margaret's eyes flicked between Roger and Anne and back again. She was a little surprised, as the ease and familiarity between them had led her to assume a different relationship.

If Anne had been Roger's fiancée, it wouldn't have surprised her at all. As it was, she was dismayed. Just as she was discovering a deep affection for John, he turned out to be James and he had a fiancée, too. Oh, well. That was the end of it, then.

She had thought there was probably no future for them, as he was from a different social class and now, here was the proof. At least he wasn't already married with children. It would do no good dreaming of what could happen when she knew it was impossible, especially now.

Ian laughed.

'I don't suppose it will come to that and

if he is returned to familiar surroundings, I'm sure that will help. Of course, we are rather assuming it is him, although that sounds more likely than not.'

'Why don't we go now and see?' Anne asked eagerly.

Roger looked at his wristwatch.

'It is getting a little late now. If it is convenient,' he said, looking at Margaret, 'can we leave him in your care until the morning?'

'Of course,' she said. 'Another night with us is no problem at all and that way we don't need to wonder if anyone has already gone to bed by the time we get back.'

'Good. Might I suggest then that we have another couple of dances and then Anne and I can run you home in the motor car. That way we will know where to find you in the morning.'

'You have a motor car?' Margaret asked. 'How lovely! I've never ridden in a motor car before. That will be very exciting.'

Mixed Feelings

Margaret was surprised when she came downstairs in the morning to find that the others were already having breakfast. Despite her late night she had thought to be up promptly and tell them her news about John/James, but hadn't set her alarm clock. Obviously it was later in the morning than she had intended.

'Ah, Margaret, good, we have something important to tell you,' her father started, rising to his feet.

'Yes, yes, Father, but we made an important discovery last night too, we . . .' She stopped as the front door knocker was heard.

'Oh gosh, here they are now!'

She turned quickly and went to open the front door as the others looked on in puzzlement. They could hear Margaret's voice saying, 'Hello, yes, please do come in,' and some murmurs in return. The other three rose from the table, leaving their napkins behind as clearly there were visitors.

The dining-room door opened again and Margaret beckoned James.

'John, John, come and see who has arrived.' James left the room followed by Margaret who put her hand on his shoulder and steered him across the hall to the parlour.

'James, thank goodness we've found you,' Anne called out as he entered, and she flung her arms around him.

'Anne, Roger!' James said, looking totally bemused.

The Reverend and Mrs Hodges stood in the doorway, looked at each other with a smile and turned again to watch the reunion.

'Thank goodness, you do remember them!' Margaret said with obvious relief. 'Now let me introduce everyone else. Father, Mrs Hodges, let me introduce Roger Radfield and Anne Harper who are the brother and fiancée of James here, that we have been calling John.

'Roger, Anne, let me introduce my father, the Reverend Preston and our housekeeper Mrs Hodges.'

They shook hands all round and the Reverend asked Mrs Hodges to make some fresh tea and invited everyone to sit down.

'They do say that timing is everything,' the Reverend said, 'and we were about to tell Margaret that James had just recovered his memory when the door knocker went.'

Margaret looked at James in amazement and he grinned back at her in a slightly sheepish way.

Anne pulled James down beside her on the sofa and Margaret felt it like a dagger stabbed into her heart. Knowing from last night that Anne and James were engaged was one thing, but seeing it in front of her, made it so much more real.

Until now it had felt as if John and James were different people; but this was the harsh reality and she felt jealousy rising up in her.

Suddenly it was now all crystal clear to her, when it should have been clear enough yesterday. She had completely fallen in love with James, but now as she realised this, she also understood that she had lost him, although perhaps she had never really had him in the first place. There was a lump in her throat, so she stood suddenly.

'I'll help Mrs Hodges,' she said quietly and left the room before anyone could notice her pain.

She stood in the hall for a few minutes to wipe the damp from her eyes, take some deep breaths and regain her composure. It was quite obvious what she had to do. She had to let James go and marry the fiancée that he loved, and who clearly loved him, without either of them guessing her feelings.

At the same time Margaret definitely had to refuse Ian because now she was quite sure she didn't love him. She was sufficiently fond of Ian to let him go, too, because he deserved to find someone who would love him in return.

She took another couple of deep breaths to steady herself and then headed for the kitchen.

Back in the Fold

By the time Margaret and Mrs Hodges got back to the parlour with the tea and some biscuits, all had been explained and Roger had written down the Radfields' address for the Reverend.

'I should point out,' the Reverend said, writing his future address on a piece of notepaper, 'that we'll be leaving here in a few weeks and moving to Cambridge, so I will give you that address and the date of the move too. We will definitely want to hear from you when James is fully recovered.'

'I have no doubt,' Roger replied, 'that our mother will be writing to you immediately to express her thanks for looking after James. When we left her she was already distressed and anxious about his apparent disappearance.

'I called her on the telephone at the hotel first thing this morning to say that we thought we had found him, but I know that she won't rest easy until she's seen him with her own eyes.'

The Reverend picked up the Radfields' address and read it.

'Westwood Hall?' he said enquiringly to Roger and James.

'Yes, it's an old house and estate just outside the village of Dullingham, south of Newmarket. Our father is an invalid now, so James runs the estate proper and I run the stud on the estate.

'If you go to Cambridge by train, you will see the house just after passing Dullingham station. It's fairly obvious, built of red brick and has tall chimneys.'

'We shall indeed be moving to Cambridge by train, so we will definitely look for it as we pass by.

'Now we mustn't delay you further, as you have a long drive ahead of you and your mother is probably on tenterhooks waiting for your return,' the Reverend said, ushering them to the door.

James, Roger and Anne came out of the manse to find a small crowd of boys standing around their car in admiration of the shining example of automotive splendour.

The few girls in the crowd nudged each other and transferred their attention to Anne as soon as she appeared. This was not a street much frequented by the rich and stylish.

'I'll drive,' Roger said to James. 'You and Anne sit in the back and you can tell Anne what you have been doing this past week.' Roger also thought that he would be more comfortable with a little distance between him and Anne as he didn't want to start giving his brother misleading ideas.

'We also need to call at the hotel, collect all of our bags and settle up before we head home.'

The crowd of children scattered to the roadside as the Radfields drove away waving to the Prestons, who were standing on the steps of the house.

Sitting in the back seat of the car, Anne turned to face a bemused looking James.

'Ian and Margaret said you had been attacked and lost your memory. I was relieved that you remembered us, it would have been quite awful if you hadn't known us this morning.'

'It was certainly a surprise for me that you appeared this morning as I had only just recovered my memory.' James kept his tongue firmly in his cheek.

It didn't seem like a big deception and one of timing more than fact. Nobody knew but him and nobody was going to question it. He had stolen a little while for himself before returning to do his duty and there were things in the war that troubled his conscience much more than that.

'If you hadn't appeared, I would have borrowed money for a ticket and been heading for the railway station in an hour or so.'

'Well thank goodness we were prompt this morning! And it was pure chance that we met Ian and Margaret at the dance last night.' Anne coloured slightly as James raised an eyebrow.

'We saw the notice for the dance quite by chance and I badgered Roger into taking me, as otherwise we would have been sitting around in the hotel with nothing to do but read the newspapers.'

James patted her hand reassuringly.

'Don't worry, I know how much you love to dance and you couldn't have resisted.'

Anne swallowed nervously as she scrutinised James's face. She noticed the yellowing bruise on his temple.

'Oh you poor dear,' she said, taking James's hand in hers and kissing the knuckles. 'I see you've still got a nasty bruise on your forehead so you must take it easy for a while even when you're back to full strength.'

'Don't worry about that,' James said, going with the distraction quite willingly. He realised he didn't really mind his brother taking his fiancée to a dance.

After all, they had had plenty of opportunity for more than that during the war, so feeling jealous or possessive at this point would be like closing the stable door after the horse had bolted.

'So how did you get hurt?' Anne asked.

'Did you see who hit you on the head?'

'I don't know, that part is still a blank. I remember leaving the pub to walk back to the hotel, but then the next bit I can remember is waking up in a strange bed with a splitting headache and wondering where on earth I was.'

'Have they no idea what happened?'

'They think somebody hit me from behind and then I fell on my face before they robbed me of my wallet and cufflinks.

'That's why I would have had to borrow money for the train because all my money and my return train ticket were gone.

'Anyway, Miss Preston found me on the steps of the Methodist chapel when she was getting ready for her Sunday school. My assailant must have dragged me there out of sight of passers-by while he robbed me.'

'Goodness, finding you there must have been a shock for her.'

'I expect it was, especially as by all accounts I was laying in a pool of my own blood.'

Anne put her hand to her mouth in horror at the picture he described.

'However, she's no shrinking violet and in the next few days nursed me until I was mostly recovered.'

James suspected that he could see a speculative gleam in Anne's eye and thought it would do no harm to deflect any suspicions that his fiancée might have.

Betraying his feelings for Margaret to Anne would be unwise for their future relationship as a married couple.

'I believe she's done the same first-aid course as you did with the Red Cross. Her fiancé is the doctor that treated me,' he clarified.

'Oh well. Good practice for a future doctor's wife, I suppose.'

'James,' Roger called from the front seat, 'I didn't think to ask the Reverend. Is there a doctor's bill I should have paid?'

'No. I did ask, but he said he was a friend of the family and so there would be no charge.'

'I must say,' Anne said, 'that you were fortunate to have fallen in with such good Samaritans. They seem to have been very kind and generous.'

'Yes, they are. I suppose we should expect that from a church minister, but it doesn't always follow,' James replied.

It occurred to him that it was kind and caring of Roger and Anne as well to come looking for him. He would expect it of Roger and James would have done the same for him if their positions were reversed.

Perhaps Anne cared for him more than he thought, as she had joined the search for him.

He felt affection for her, which was a rather lukewarm basis to start life together, but maybe it would be enough for the marriage to work.

'Oh, before I forget,' Roger said, 'I made enquiries among a couple of your old soldiers in case they knew where you might be. One of them was an unemployed ex-groom living in Cheveley.

'He said you'd offered jobs to any men that had no work and as he was a groom before the war I've taken him on in the stud.'

'Thank you. What's his name?'

'It's a private who said he lost an arm in late 1917 and he's been unemployed and living with his parents since. Name of Benson.'

'Benson!' James exclaimed. 'I thought I'd seen the last of him.'

'Did I do wrong?'

'No, I did offer work to all of them that needed it. Unfortunately Benson is who the Duke of Wellington had in mind a hundred years ago when he described his common soldiers as 'the scum of the earth'. Just tell your stable master to keep a close eye on him.'

'I will do. He'll be on trial for a month anyway.'

When James arrived home his parents were greatly relieved his assault did not appear to have caused any lasting damage other than to Lady Radfield's damp handkerchiefs.

His grateful mother immediately wrote a letter of thanks to the Reverend and in it promised to visit them soon.

A Wedding Surprise

'That was a surprise,' the Reverend said as they stood on the steps of the manse, waving to the Radfields driving away. 'And now we have another surprise for you, Margaret.'

'Oh, what is that?' Margaret said as she stopped waving and turned towards the house, looking curiously at her father who was grinning in a rather uncharacteristic way.

'Come inside and you'll find out,' he replied, ushering the other two back into the house.

They went into the dining-room to finish their interrupted breakfast.

'Before anyone else comes to the door,' the Reverend said, taking Mrs Hodges' hand, 'we have something to tell you.'

Margaret looked at their joined hands and her eyebrows rose. She looked up to see her father and Mrs Hodges gazing into each other's eyes and smiling. They turned back to face Margaret.

'I've asked Mrs Hodges to marry me and she has accepted,' the Reverend said.

Margaret's surprise was complete and her mouth dropped open. Then she squealed in delight and flung her arms around Mrs Hodges and then her father.

'That's wonderful news! I was so sad to think of leaving you behind,' she said to Mrs Hodges excitedly. 'I'm so happy that you'll be coming with us. When, do tell, when are you getting married? Can I be your bridesmaid?'

'Well, we had wondered,' her father said, glancing at Mrs Hodges and then at Margaret, 'if there might be the possibility of two weddings?'

Margaret's excitement evaporated suddenly. She hadn't told anybody yet of her decision because it had only become completely clear to her an hour ago when Roger, and most particularly Anne, had been there.

She paused for a moment to gather her thoughts, while her father and his new fiancée waited expectantly. Margaret was sure that they were going to be disappointed when she told them.

However there was nothing to be gained by delay or prevaricating, especially as Ian was likely to be at the door any time soon. She took a deep breath and looked up to face the other two.

'I have to turn him down.' She shook her head sadly. 'I like Ian, but not enough . . . and marriage is for your whole life. I can't do it.'

The Reverend's shoulders sagged a little and Mrs Hodges stepped forward and put her arms around Margaret in a gentle embrace.

Just then the front door knocker sounded and Margaret stiffened, sure it was Ian. She didn't want to do this, but she had no choice.

Mrs Hodges hugged Margaret gently and said quietly.

'Be brave. You go into the parlour while I see to the door.'

Mrs Hodges turned towards the door to the hall and caught the Reverend's elbow before he could go and answer the front door.

'You stay here, Reverend, and finish your breakfast. No doubt that is Dr Gordon come to see Margaret. We'll call you if you're needed.'

'Er, yes, of course,' the Reverend said, hesitating before moving back to the table.

Mrs Hodges went into the hall and waited for Margaret to pass by her into the parlour before opening the front door.

'Good morning, doctor,' she said brightly to Ian who was indeed waiting on the step, 'have you come to see Margaret?'

'Yes, I have. I'm not too early, am I?' he asked as he stepped inside and removed his hat.

'No, not at all. She's in the parlour,' Mrs Hodges replied as she took his hat and put it on the hall table. 'However, you've just missed John, or rather James, your patient, who left ten minutes ago with his brother and fiancée.'

'Ah, so he was indeed the missing

brother, then. I'm glad we have that mystery sorted out,' he said to her as he stepped into the parlour. Mrs Hodges closed the door quietly behind him.

Margaret was standing nervously in the middle of the carpet, her hands clasped in front of her, her teeth gently biting her lower lip.

Ian was not really surprised to see her looking nervous and strode across to stand in front of her, taking her trembling hands in his.

'Good morning, Margaret,' he said, smiling at her. 'Do you have an answer for me?'

She swallowed and dropped her gaze to study his jacket while she plucked up the courage to say what had to be said. She drew a deep breath.

'I'm sorry Ian, but I can't marry you,' she said quietly. She looked up to meet his eyes that had opened wide.

'You're a good man and I'm fond of you, but not enough to marry you.' She squeezed his hands.

'You deserve someone that will love

you wholeheartedly and I like you well enough to want that for you. But that someone isn't me. I'm so sorry.'

Ian stood very still and there was silence as he searched her face where her eyes were glistening as she tried to hold back tears.

'I thought . . . perhaps with a little time?' He faltered to a stop, holding her hands to his chest.

'No, Ian, there's no more time,' she said, 'and it's best if we stop now.' She leaned forward and kissed him lightly on the cheek before pulling her hands from his as she moved back.

Ian sighed.

'I'm sorry. I had hopes . . .' His voice trailed off.

'I'm sorry too, but I'll soon be gone and we both need to move on.'

She stepped forward towards the door, not wanting to prolong the awkwardness and he turned and walked beside her into the hall where he picked up his hat.

Margaret opened the front door and he stepped into the doorway.

'Please thank your father for all his hospitality and that I wish him well at his new church in Cambridge.' He put his hat on his head and stepped outside.

'I will. Goodbye, Ian.' She closed the door and stood there facing it while two tears rolled down her cheeks.

Reaching into her pocket for a handkerchief she turned and found herself walking into the embrace of Mrs Hodges, who had silently materialised behind her.

Margaret's thoughts and emotions were in complete turmoil. In the space of an hour or two, she thought, she had realised whom she loved and lost him; realised whom she didn't love and probably lost him as a friend, too; and found out she was gaining a stepmother.

She let the tears flow for a moment to get her emotions back under control.

Margaret imagined that Mrs Hodges thought the tears were just for Ian and didn't realise they were mostly for James but that it was best that Mrs Hodges keep thinking it was so.

Margaret straightened up and blew

her nose.

'I think we need to get busy,' Mrs Hodges said, 'there are breakfast things to clear away, unless you're still hungry, beds to make, lunch to start and we still have one wedding to plan.'

Margaret nodded and put her handkerchief away.

'I can't keep calling you Mrs Hodges, can I? At least, not for much longer. What shall I call you?'

Mrs Hodges thought for a moment.

'What seems right? What would you like to call me?'

Margaret's forehead frowned for a moment and then her face cleared.

'Do you suppose . . . I'm not sure if it would be right . . .' She frowned again and hesitated for a moment.

'For years you have felt much like a mother to me. Would it be proper if I called you Mother?'

Mrs Hodges' face broke into a broad smile.

'I would be very happy for you to call me Mother and I always wanted a child of my own. I'm sure it would be no disrespect to your real mother and I can't imagine your father objecting.'

She leaned forward and kissed Margaret on the cheek as Margaret's face relaxed into a smile too.

'It's best if we get busy, so shall we?' After lunch, the three of them sat in the parlour and discussed the wedding. It was decided to have the wedding soon, in the chapel next door and before the move to Cambridge so that all their friends in Ipswich could attend.

Doing so would also stop any speculative gossip if people knew Mrs Hodges was going to Cambridge as well.

Margaret was excited at the prospect of being a bridesmaid and she and Mrs Hodges insisted that 'soon' had to be at least a couple of weeks as they had wedding clothes to make.

They also agreed that it was not a good time for the newlyweds to go away, so the Reverend said he would write to his sister in Brighton.

He would invite her to the wedding,

and also ask if Margaret could return with her after the wedding for a fortnight and then that would give the newlyweds a little time on their own.

A Crushing Blow
for James

A month after James's return home, he was back to full fitness and his mother decided that the time was right for her to go to Ipswich and thank the Prestons in person.

'James,' Lady Radfield said one morning at breakfast, 'I shall write to the Reverend Preston this morning. I have it in mind to visit him on Friday to thank him in person. Will you come with me?'

James drank his cup of tea slowly as he considered his reply. He still thought of Margaret nearly every day and the pain and heartache of losing her didn't seem to be going away.

Whether she was already married or not, seeing her again could only make it worse. On the other hand he owed the Prestons a great deal and he was obliged to visit and thank them properly sooner or later.

'Yes, Mother, I'll come with you on Friday. We shouldn't leave it any longer.

'If you will excuse me now, I have much to do today.' James knew that dwelling on the visit would do no good and that he should keep himself busy.

Lady Radfield peered over her reading glasses at James as he stood and left the breakfast room. She turned to her husband.

'George, I notice James seems to be working very hard recently. Is there an unusual amount of work to do on the estate at the moment?'

'No. Not that I am aware of anyway. If you ask me, there's something bothering him since he went to that army reunion, but I'm blessed if I know what it is. Perhaps it reminded him of friends who didn't come home.'

They looked at each other in silence for a minute or two before Lady Radfield's eyes flicked back to the door where James had made his exit.

* * *

James was perfectly well aware of why he was working hard. Keeping busy all the time was the only way to keep his mind from dwelling on Anne and Margaret.

He knew that he and Anne were expected to marry. They had been engaged for quite long enough.

However, he also knew that he no longer had any enthusiasm to marry her. The reason was clear. He had lost his heart to Margaret but she was marrying someone else. He supposed he could do his duty and marry Anne but was that foolish?

He liked Anne and had affection for her, but that's all it was these days. Was that really enough for marriage?

Would love grow back or would it all simply fall apart?

He didn't want to hurt Anne by rejecting her after all this time, but he didn't want to hurt her more with a loveless marriage, so he didn't know what to do.

Had he ever really loved Anne? Or was it simply an infatuation that had got out of hand?

He just didn't know any more and didn't want to do anything stupid that he couldn't take back. It was an agonising situation and his head was just going around and around with it.

* * *

On Friday, after an early lunch, James joined his mother in the car for the journey to Ipswich.

He was feeling anxious about how he would react when they got to the Reverend's house. He would be pleased to see the Reverend and Mrs Hodges again.

He wasn't sure how he would react to Margaret. He knew he would be pleased to see her once more even though it was sure to cause him heartache. He would just have to make sure it didn't show.

He considered the possibility that she was already married and living with the doctor and wouldn't even be there.

Then again, he thought, they knew he and his mother were visiting today and the doctor and Margaret might make a point of calling to see them. It was just too complicated and James resolved to stop thinking about it and guessing what might happen. He would find out when he got there.

'Tell me again about the Prestons, James, and where they live,' his mother said, providing a welcome interruption.

James noticed that his mother was a little nervous at the prospect of meeting them. James occupied himself by putting her fears to rest by telling her about the family, the house and how they lived in a perfectly respectable part of town.

Lady Radfield and James arrived at the manse in Ipswich in the early afternoon. The chauffeur assisted her ladyship from the car while James rang the doorbell.

It was answered by Mrs Hodges, except that she was no longer Mrs Hodges but Mrs Preston, the marriage having taken place the week before.

Mrs Preston opened the door, to find James and an elegant and expensively dressed lady following him up the steps. The new Mrs Preston had advance warning of the visit, so she was wearing her Sunday best and had cleaned and tidied the house so that it was immaculate.

'Good afternoon, Lady Radfield, please come in,' she said, stepping to the side and smiling a welcome at James as the Reverend came down the hall.

Lady Radfield stepped forward to shake the hand of the Reverend.

'Reverend Preston, I'm very pleased to meet you, I hope I'm not inconveniencing you?'

'Not at all, it is very kind of you to visit us, may I take your hat and coat?' the Reverend replied.

'Thank you,' she said, pulling out the pin from her hat so that she could remove it.

Mrs Preston took her hat and coat and asked if she would care for some tea while the Reverend shook James's hand.

'That would be lovely,' Lady Radfield said, 'this long dry summer and the journey has left my throat is quite parched.'

'Do step into the parlour,' the Reverend said, opening the door and ushering her in, 'and James can tell us how he is getting on now he is recovered.' Lady Radfield went in and sat on the sofa, looking around her with approval as she did so. Her family had always been Church of England and she wasn't entirely sure what to expect in a Methodist minister's house.

She was very class conscious and immediately saw that it was, as James had said, very respectable middle class. It was not unlike the vicarage in her village.

James joined her on the sofa, wondering where Margaret was.

'I've heard a great deal about you from James,' his mother said, 'and my husband and I are both very grateful to you for the way that you took him in and looked after him.'

'It was a pleasure,' the Reverend said, 'it was no trouble at all and James was very good company for us.'

'I must thank you as well,' James said. 'My departure was so sudden, I'm not sure that I thanked you properly.

'If I had been carted off to the hospital I might still be there now. Then we wouldn't have had the good fortune for Margaret and Roger to have crossed paths at the dance and realise who I was.'

Lady Radfield glanced sideways at James and he remembered that his mother had been given an edited version of how Roger had found him. Roger taking Anne to a dance when they were supposed to be looking for James was not something that she was likely to approve of. He decided a change of topic was required.

Fortunately, Mrs Preston chose that moment to come into the room with the tea things. Everything had been ready in the kitchen and she had only needed to pour water into the teapot.

'I understand you have a daughter,' Lady Radfield said.

'Yes indeed, but she's gone down to Brighton for a couple of weeks following the wedding,' the Reverend replied.

The Reverend and Mrs Preston gave each other a little smile.

Now James knew. She had married the doctor and it was definitely all at an end. He had not wanted to admit to himself that there was a tiny corner of his heart still hoping they might have some sort of future.

Finally there was nothing more that could be said or done. His flimsy hopes had turned to ash.

'I gather that James runs your estate and your son Roger runs your stud. Presumably the demand for horses has dropped now the war has ended?' the Reverend asked.

'Yes, indeed, it has been quite difficult. We anticipated the end of the war to a certain extant, but horses take eleven months to foal, so you can't just switch things off.

'There's not much demand for carriage horses at the moment and I doubt it will improve now people are buying motor cars. We've always bred racehorses and hacks too, so I think we may have to concentrate on that side now.'

The conversation continued for a little longer and James saw that his mother had relaxed.

She obviously agreed that Prestons were, as James had said, perfectly amiable and acceptable people living in a respectable part of town.

Lady Radfield announced that it was time for them to leave if they were to arrive home before dark.

'I should like to visit you again if I may, once you have moved to Cambridge as it will be much closer and easier to reach.'

'We will be delighted to see you again and you will be very welcome. We shall be there in only a couple of weeks now.

'No doubt James explained that Methodist ministers move around every few years and I've always wanted to go back to Cambridge where I spent several years when I was a student.'

'It's a lovely city and very easy for us to reach by train,' Lady Radfield said as she stood and started to put her gloves on again.

Mrs Preston stood as well and went to retrieve their hats and coats.

'Will you be travelling from here to

Cambridge by train?' Lady Radfield asked.

'Yes, we will be sending most of our things in advance with a carrier and then following on a day later by train,' the Reverend replied.

'In that case look carefully to the east as you leave Dullingham station and you will see our house,' Lady Radfield said as Mrs Preston helped her to don her coat.

'It's clearly visible through the trees and is no more than half a mile from the station.'

'We shall definitely look out for it as we pass,' the Reverend said as he moved to open the front door.

'Thank you so much for coming to see us and we shall look forward to seeing you in Cambridge.'

They all shook hands and the Prestons waved as James and his mother drove away.

'James,' his mother said as the car turned the corner at the end of the street, 'we were obliged to call, but to be honest

I hadn't been quite sure what to expect. I know you said they were respectable and educated people, and they are, but I hadn't expected to find them so very agreeable. I shall look forward to visiting them in Cambridge.'

No Easy Answers

Anne, James's fiancée, lived with her widowed father, Sir John Harper, on the northern side of Newmarket. Her brother had died in the trenches some three years previously.

Her elder sister had married before the war and now lived in Norwich with her husband and two small children.

It was a quiet afternoon and Anne had come into the calm and peace of the garden. She sat in the afternoon shade of an old oak tree to read a novel.

However, she had been stuck on the same page for at least half an hour now and she simply couldn't concentrate on it, as her mind kept drifting to the Radfields.

She and James had become betrothed several years ago while James was on leave from the army. They had met a few months before the war started and it was probably her brother's death and

James's experiences in the trenches that had focused their minds and led to their engagement.

Now, since several months ago, James was back and it was time to think about the wedding. Lady Radfield had been hinting heavily about dates and how it was preferable to hold weddings in warm weather and how winter was approaching.

The difficulty was that Anne no longer wanted to marry James. It had all seemed a little chaotic before, as James hadn't been released from the army until just before Easter. Now they had been able to spend much more time together, she realised her feelings had changed.

Not only that, but the time spent with Roger, while they were looking for James, made it clear to her that Roger was now the one she loved.

That it was James's brother, just made things worse and she felt very guilty because it was like a betrayal of James. She wasn't even sure when or why the change had happened. It might have been while she was visiting Lady Radfield, as she had done frequently during the war.

James had been away but Roger had been there all the time producing horses for the army. Perhaps James had changed during the war; perhaps she was the one who had changed while he was away.

They say that absence makes the heart grow fonder but they also say that untended fires go out. Anne thought wryly it was fortunate there so many sayings to choose from, since you could always find an appropriate one.

Anne sat in the wicker armchair frowning. It was a real dilemma and she didn't know what to do. Everybody expected her to marry James.

How could she tell her war hero she was dumping him after they had been engaged for years? Nobody would understand and she would get all kinds of pressure to go through with it, especially from her father and his mother.

Even if she called a halt to it, she was going to lose the friendship of Roger as well, because she would have no reason to be still visiting Westwood Hall.

Lady Radfield had become a friend over the last few years and losing her companionship would be a wrench, too. As well, her ladyship would probably be angry at Anne for breaking an engagement that had lasted so long. Anne's life would be a complete misery.

She was sure Roger regarded her with affection, but most likely as a sister-in-law, not as a potential wife. She simply couldn't marry James whom she didn't love and then keep crossing paths with Roger that she did love, as that would drive her crazy.

The alternative was not to marry James and not to see Roger ever again and that was almost, but perhaps not quite, as bad.

Her eyes filled with tears and she absentmindedly wiped them away with her lace handkerchief.

If only she could talk to someone about it. Her mother and brother were gone; her father wouldn't understand and she wasn't sure this was something she could even discuss with him anyway. Her sister was far away and this was something which couldn't be discussed in a letter. If only her mother was still here.

Lady Radfield had become a substitute mother in many ways but obviously she was the last person Anne could consult. That made Anne realise yet again that if she gave up James she would be giving up his mother, too, who had become such a great friend over the last few years. Anne wiped away fresh tears. The future was looking bleak.

Having eliminated the other possibilities, Anne realised that her only choice was her sister and she would have to visit her in Norwich. She had to write her a note asking if she could visit her and very soon.

Anne felt a little better now that she had a plan of sorts, so she took a deep shuddering breath, wiped her eyes, closed the novel and rose from her chair, heading for the writing desk in her bedroom. As she entered the house, she met Johnson, their butler, coming in the other direction carrying a letter on a silver salver.

'The post has just arrived and there is a letter for you, miss.'

'Thank you, Johnson,' she replied, picking up the letter and continuing past him. She looked at the envelope as she climbed the stairs and with a sinking heart recognised the handwriting of Lady Radfield.

Anne sat at her writing desk and looked again at the envelope with a sigh. No doubt it was a summons to Westwood Hall. She couldn't ignore it or pretend it hadn't come, so she took out the letter and unfolded the single sheet.

She was right. It was a summons. A politely worded invitation to lunch next Sunday, but nevertheless a summons.

Anne let the letter fall on to the desk and rested her forehead on her hand while she wondered what she could do.

The answer, she realised after a moment, was to write to her sister, not to ask for an invitation but simply to say that she was on her way. Her sister might be irritated if she had other plans, but she wasn't going to refuse when Anne turned up on her doorstep.

That way she could now send an apology to Lady Radfield saying that she was just about to visit her sister for two, or . . . no, three weeks.

No doubt there would be another invitation to Westwood Hall when she got back, but at least it put the crisis off for almost a month. She hoped her sister would have good advice or at least help her to find the strength and determination to do something positive.

Anne sat forward and reached for pen and paper. If she was prompt she could catch the afternoon post and her sister and Lady Radfield would both have their letters tomorrow morning.

Then all she needed to do was pack a bag ready to go tomorrow on the morning train. She would be in Norwich by lunchtime. Her sister should have got the post by then and could meet her with the car at the station.

Three weeks later, after long chats with her sister, Anne was clear in her mind. She couldn't marry James, and it would be a big mistake to do so. This would mean parting from Roger and Lady Radfield too, but it was the only sensible thing to do.

Anne was going to be miserable for a long time, but a busy life was going to be the only answer.

Anne had helped with the Red Cross during the war and also joined the new Women's Institute, but had left both at the end, expecting to get married and start a new family. She planned to throw herself back into them with all the energy and time she could find and put the Radfields behind her.

A Daunting Decision

James had been home for two months now. As far as he could tell, he was as fit as he could be but he knew that everything wasn't the same as it was before he had gone to Ipswich.

Since he had been back, he had been restless. He had thrown himself into work on the estate and surprised some of the estate workers by turning up beside them to do some of the manual work. But hard physical labour fixing fences and gathering wheat into stooks was still giving him too much time to think.

At the end of the month he was sitting at his desk, supposedly going over the estate accounts. His mind wasn't on it and he finally admitted the truth to himself. He didn't love Anne. He wasn't sure if it had ever been more than a wartime infatuation.

Now he had fallen in love with Margaret. But Margaret had married Ian and

184

James couldn't possibly meet her again.

Now he had to step away from Anne and get on with his life. In some ways it was a bleak prospect, but at least he had Roger and his parents for company and the estate to keep him busy. Sooner or later Roger was bound to meet someone to marry and then start a family. That way his parents would get the grandchildren and heirs that they yearned for.

Anne was coming for lunch on Sunday and he simply had to end it then. Gentlemen weren't supposed to break engagements but he must. He would have to ask her to forgive him for keeping her hanging on. He sighed and rubbed his face. He knew his mother and Anne had become close during the years he was away and his mother was definitely going to be upset.

Sunday lunch at Westwood Hall was a strained affair. James and Anne were barely speaking beyond civilities and pleasantries. Lady Radfield was becoming irritated with the pair of them.

Her principle reason for inviting Anne

today was to push her and James into naming the day, because their engagement was dragging on and on. It was past time that her two sons got married and produced some grandchildren.

James had at least got engaged but now seemed to be in no hurry to actually get married. She had spent the last hour asking leading questions that were consistently evaded by the pair of them and dropping hints that were also continually ignored by both Anne and James. Her husband, never a great conversationalist, was keeping quiet, too. An uncomfortable silence was falling on the table.

Roger was feeling depressed and not at all talkative. Anne's appearance at Westwood Hall that morning had stirred uncomfortable feelings in him. He had finally understood that his affection for Anne was not sisterly but something more.

When she was married to James and living in the same house, it was going to be intolerable for him. He would have to leave. He thought perhaps he could go to Canada or Australia. As soon as lunch was over he needed to escape and the atmosphere was so tense he didn't think he would be missed.

'Mother,' Roger said, 'if you don't mind I would prefer to skip coffee. I feel I need to get some fresh air and exercise, so I'm inclined to go for a ride.'

Lady Radfield sighed with resignation.

'Yes, Roger, do that, I think some air would be a good idea for all of you. James, I'm going to take a nap, so why don't you take Anne out into the rose garden?'

'Shall we do that, Anne?' James asked. Anne looked up at him to see that he seemed less than enchanted to be with her in the seclusion of the rose garden. But she knew that she had to tell him it was over. It was best to get it done and in private.

After, she could find her chauffeur and leave quietly before Lady Radfield and Roger reappeared.

She doubted that Lady Radfield was really taking a nap but James could tell her the engagement was broken while she went home to tell her father.

She rose from the table and headed quickly for the French windows. Anne didn't wait for James; she knew the way from so many visits over the years and wanted to get her emotions under control before anyone saw her face.

James told the maid to take coffee for two to the rose garden and then he lingered in the house. He didn't relish being interrupted by a maid delivering coffee in the middle of him telling Anne he couldn't marry her.

Eventually he went out to the rose garden and found Anne sitting in one of two wicker armchairs, sipping coffee. His coffee was already on the wicker table between the chairs. After all, she knew how he took his coffee. As he approached, Anne glanced up and gave him a faint and trembling smile. His smile in return was equally weak.

'I've poured your coffee, don't let it get cold,' she said to him as he sat in the other chair.

'Anne, we need to talk about our engagement,' James said, not being able to wait any longer and ignoring the coffee. He sat in the armchair but looked across the garden into the distance, not at Anne.

'The war was a bloody affair and we all did and saw things we can't even talk about. Some of it was so horrifying that we can't bear to think about it now.'

Anne stared at his face with her mouth slightly open in surprise.

'The war changed us. It changed me. I'm not the same person that you got engaged to, so very long ago and I don't think it would be right for us to marry now. I think you should call off the engagement.' He finally turned and looked into her eyes.

'Can we just be friends for now and get to know each other again? Then if we want to, in a few months time, we could get engaged again and start afresh.'

Anne just stared at him for a few moments more and then reached over, put her hand on his forearm and gave him a trembling smile.

'You don't know how relieved I am! I've thought for several weeks that getting married just now would be a mistake and I've been terrified of telling you.'

Now it was James's turn to stare at Anne.

'Really? Gosh! I never expected you to say that.' The surprise on James's face gradually changed to a relieved smile. 'I'm sorry I was so grumpy today, but I didn't want to hurt you and I've been dreading saying it. I'm sure I haven't slept properly for the last week.'

'Just a week? Shame on you!' She tapped his arm gently as a mild reproach 'I've been agonising over this for the last two months. I even went to visit my sister in Norwich for three weeks to have someone to talk to about it!'

'Well, while you were agonising I've been throwing myself into work on the estate so as not to be thinking too much, but it didn't help.'

'You poor thing!' Anne said, relief now clearly audible in her voice. 'We've both been torturing ourselves about the same thing and for no reason. Now I wish we had spoken about it before. Well, we can both relax now and go back to being just good friends.' She paused for a moment. 'Except for one small thing.'

'One small thing?'

'Yes, drink your coffee and then we have to tell your mother. She is definitely not going to like it. At least this way we can give each other moral support.'

James groaned.

'This is very true,' he said. 'I suppose we must, but why don't we sit out here a little longer?'

'Don't be a chicken,' Anne said indignantly.

James gave a her a sly grin, drained his cup and rose, offering Anne his arm. She realised he had been kidding, pursed her lips and kicked him gently on his shoe before taking his arm.

They strolled back across the lawn, arm in arm and smiling.

'Oh dear,' Anne said, the smile slipping from her face. 'I can see your mother lurking just inside the French windows. I bet she's just jumped to the wrong conclusion.'

'So much for the nap. She probably thinks we just named the day. We had better get this over with and tell her before she has a chance to make any plans.'

James and Anne entered the drawing room to find his mother standing, smiling, by the fireplace.

'Well, my dears,' she said as they drew near, 'have you something to tell me at last?'

'Yes, Mother,' James replied, 'but it's not what you are expecting.' James looked at Anne standing next to him. She put her hand on his forearm and smiled at him reassuringly. They both turned back to face Lady Radfield who was starting to look puzzled.

'Mother . . .' James started nervously, 'we have decided not to get married. We both think it's for the best and the right thing to do.'

Lady Radfield stared at them in horror.

'Not get married?' she whispered. She reached for a nearby armchair and, trembling, sat down.

'No, Mother, I'm afraid we've broken off our engagement,' James confirmed. 'We're sorry to disappoint you, but we both realise that we don't wish to marry each other any more.'

Lady Radfield's face crumpled and she put her hands to her face as tears started to roll down her cheeks.

'But I was so looking forward to it. You make such a lovely couple.' Her shoulders shook as she started sobbing in earnest.

James stepped forward hesitantly, half raising his hand but unsure what to do.

Anne stepped past him, knelt on the floor next to the armchair and put her arms around Lady Radfield who let her tears flow into Anne's shoulder. Anne looked back at James and made flicking motions with her fingers. James took the hint and went out of the French windows to sit on the terrace and wait for the storm to pass.

Twenty minutes later Anne came out and sat in the chair next to him. He looked at her enquiringly.

'She's still a bit upset,' Anne said, 'but now she really has gone upstairs to lie down.'

James reached for her hand and squeezed it gently.

'Thank you, Anne, I do appreciate your help. It would have been difficult without you.'

Anne squeezed his hand back.

'That's quite all right, I couldn't just leave the two of you on your own. I confess I meant to, but in the end I couldn't run out on my friends, could I?' She give James a wry smile.

'However, it is time I was going and I'm sure you can manage to tell your father and Roger on your own while I go home and tell my father as well.'

They stood and hugged each other gently.

'Now remember,' James said, 'don't be a stranger. We're still friends and I still want you to visit fairly often.'

'I will, I promise. I just hope your mother doesn't get any ideas,' Anne said, embracing him briefly again.

He escorted her to the front door.

'I really mean it, I hope we will still see you from time to time,' James said, handing her her hat.

'Of course,' she said and kissed him on the cheek. 'Tell your mother I'll come and see her next week. Goodbye, James.' She turned quickly, putting on her hat so that James would not see the tear in her eye.

James reached past her and opened the door.

'Goodbye, Anne,' he said with a tight throat as she ran down the steps to where the chauffeur was holding the car door open for her. James watched as they drove away and then went in search of his father and Roger.

'It's a pity, I really liked her, she's a nice gel,' James's father merely commented. 'I wondered what it was all about at lunch.'

James left his father to nap in his wheelchair and went in search of Roger.

He found him in the stables grimly rubbing down a rather sweaty horse.

'Roger, there's something I need to tell you.'

Roger paused and looked up, a grim expression on his face. He wondered how the day could get worse.

'Anne and I decided to break off our engagement. It was the right thing to do.' Roger was shocked.

'Good grief, James,' he said as he stood up straight and stared at his brother. 'What happened? Did you break it off or was it Anne?'

Roger had a guilty fear that dancing in Ipswich was going to be mentioned.

'Both, really,' James said wryly. 'We had both realised a while ago that we didn't want to marry but it took us both quite a while to pluck up the courage and say something. It's ironic that as soon as we did, we discovered that the other didn't want to go through with it, either.'

Roger's black mood suddenly evaporated.

'It's just as well you discovered it now,

not after the wedding.'

'Yes, thank goodness, it's huge weight off my mind. She's still going to come from time to time as we agreed we're still friends.

'She's become quite chummy with Mother, so will visit now and again, but nobody should read anything deeper into it. By the way, I've been meaning to ask you. How's Benson getting on in the stable?'

'Benson? He's had a couple of warnings. It seems he has a tendency to slack off if you're not behind him all the time and he drinks too much. He needs to make more of an effort if he wants to stay here.'

James nodded thoughtfully before he turned and started walking slowly back to the house.

An equally thoughtful Roger also turned back slowly to continue rubbing down the horse. Then he paused, straightened up and looked towards James, who hadn't gone far.

'James,' he called.

197

James stopped and faced Roger.

'Would you . . .' Roger hesitated, searching for the right words. 'Would it be awkward for you if I were to see Anne? I mean, for example, take her to a dance or the theatre or whatever?

'I don't want you to think we've been doing anything behind your back or something, but we've always got on well and I'm unattached at the moment. It would be nice to go with someone, a friend, now and again.'

Roger came to a uncertain halt, not being quite sure what more to say, or expect to hear from his brother.

James stepped forward and clapped Roger on his shoulder.

'No, that's fine. I don't have any problem at all with that. I'm happy with it and it will be better if Anne still feels welcome here. She is coming to see Mother in a few days anyway, when the dust has settled, so be sure to catch her then.'

'Thanks, I'll do that.' Roger turned again to the horse and continued rubbing it down. He was relieved for several reasons. Firstly, his brother hadn't blamed him for ending the engagement. Secondly he didn't need to emigrate now. Thirdly he was free to court Anne, even though he hadn't expressed it that way to James.

Suddenly the day seemed much brighter. He just had to hope that Anne might be receptive to being courted by her ex-fiancé's brother. He forgot all about Benson.

A Vicious Attack

James was well aware that Roger and Anne were seeing each other and he was glad. Whilst his heart still felt as if it had a Margaret-shaped hole, at least he didn't feel stressed about having to marry Anne.

His parents, particularly his mother, appeared to have accepted that the engagement was over. He suspected that his mother hadn't quite accepted it until Anne and Roger started going out together.

He was relieved that Anne, not really wanting to marry him, had moved on and was now seeing Roger instead. After seeing them together more than once, he had a suspicion that things might progress to something more serious than a casual friendship. He was quite relaxed and happy at the idea that Anne might become a sister-in-law one day, rather than his wife.

All in all, apart from a constant sensation of loss, James was now thinking that he could cope with what life threw at him. There were times when he would be busy working when something, and he didn't know what it was, would suddenly trigger a memory of his days in Ipswich, followed by a black moment of despair. Fortunately they didn't seem to last long and he hoped that they would fade with time or become less frequent. When he compared it with some of the horrors still suffered by a few of his fellow soldiers, he thought that he shouldn't feel too sorry for himself.

★　★　★

One afternoon, after lunch, James wandered down to the stud to see a new foal. It was a pleasant tranquil afternoon and he was in no hurry to get back to his office. Anne had joined them for lunch and she and Roger were still talking to his parents. All of the grooms were still on their lunchtime break.

James walked slowly along the row of stalls, the only noises being the shuffling movement of horses and the sound of hay being chewed. The stall he was looking for was the third from the far end and as he passed along the row, a few horses stuck their heads over the top of the stable door to see who was passing.

Arriving at the right stall, James rested his arms on top of the door and watched as the mare suckled the foal, its tail swishing with pleasure.

Suddenly there was a scream from the direction of the house.

'James! Look out!'

James turned his head to look that way, as a glancing blow hit the side of his head and he fell to the ground unconscious.

Roger and Anne had been walking leisurely down to the stud, intending to go for a ride. Anne took her gloves from her pocket and started to draw them on when Roger suddenly realised he had left his behind.

'Oh, stupid of me! I left my gloves on

the hall table. Carry on and I'll catch up,' he said, before hurrying back to the house.

Anne continued down to the stables and as she rounded the corner, she saw James near the far end looking into one of the stalls. Behind him was a man with a raised piece of timber in his hand, clearly about to strike James.

'James! Look out!' she screamed and started to run towards them.

As he turned towards her, the man, Benson, struck James a blow on the head and James fell heavily on to the hard surface of the stableyard.

Benson looked up and saw Anne running towards him. He struck James again on the back with the length of timber before noticing that Roger was also running his way and not far behind Anne.

Benson kicked James in the side and turned to run away – straight into the arms of the stablemaster who wrestled him to the ground. Three more grooms and Roger arrived and Benson was pinned to the ground face down.

Anne was kneeling beside James.

'Oh James, no! Not again!' She looked up at the grooms. 'You,' she said, pointing to one of them, 'run to the house and tell them to phone for the doctor.'

'And you,' Roger said, pointing to a second groom, 'run down into the village and get the constable, while you,' he said pointing to the third man, 'go and get a length of rope to tie this one up.'

Roger took the opportunity of resting a knee in Benson's back to put his full weight on it and Benson groaned in pain, much to Roger's satisfaction.

'You ungrateful devil. I bet it was you in Ipswich too, wasn't it? We find you a job and this is how you thank us.'

'Toffs!' Benson almost spat. 'If it weren't for you there wouldn't have been no war, I wouldn't have lost my arm and lost my job, too. Pity we didn't do for the oh-so-noble major properly the first time. Give me a job? I don't need your flaming pity and you were going to sack me anyway.'

Roger looked at his stablemaster who

nodded confirmation that he was about to sack Benson.

The third groom reappeared with a length of rope in his hands. As Roger took the rope from him he was dumbfounded for a moment. He couldn't tie Benson's arms behind him because he only had one arm.

He settled for tying his ankles together, then his wrist before tying the rope around Benson's belt. Benson wasn't going anywhere before the constable got here.

The stablemaster and the groom dragged Benson well away from James and then dumped him heavily on the hard ground. This elicited more cursing from Benson, but the other two just nodded to each other in satisfaction.

Roger turned his attention to his brother. Anne had removed her jacket, folded it and placed it under James's head.

'How is he?'

'Knocked out, but I don't see any bleeding. I hope he doesn't lose his memory again.'

'At least this time we'll know who he is and where he is.' The grooms improvised a stretcher with horse blankets and carried James back to the house. They hadn't even arrived before James groaned and opened his eyes, seeing Roger walking beside him.

'Roger, what . . . ?' James said, looking around in confusion.

'Just rest there, James, while we carry you to your room. Benson bashed you on the head, but I'm glad to see you do remember me this time.'

Time to Say Goodbye

The day had come when the Prestons were to leave Ipswich for Cambridge and Margaret had mixed emotions as she looked out of her bedroom window.

This was the last time she would see this view and she wanted to fix it in her memory. It wasn't a grand panorama, just the front garden and the houses opposite, but she had been here six years, and it was her room, and her view, and now everything was going to change.

She felt sad to be leaving what felt like her only home. She didn't really remember the previous house very well. They had come here when she was a gawky, nervous schoolgirl and everything had seemed strange and a bit scary.

Now she was going to leave all her friends behind and start again. It was a little scary again, but exciting too, and she wasn't a nervous schoolgirl any more.

Her friends had grown up as she had

and a couple of them were already married. She could have stayed here and been married too, to Ian, but she knew that wasn't the answer. The answer had left and gone home with his fiancée.

She took a deep breath, wiped a tear from her eye and sighed, not sure if the tear was because she was leaving or because he had left. Perhaps both.

It was time to move on, both physically and emotionally, so she stood up straight, took a last sad glance through the window and went downstairs. Their suitcases and a picnic basket were waiting by the front door.

'Goodness,' Margaret said as she emerged with them into the street. 'It's one of those new motor taxis.'

'Yes, miss,' the cabbie answered as he loaded their suitcases and bags into the space next to the driver's seat. 'It's a brand new Napier, this is,' he said with pride in his voice. 'Nobody wants the horses now and besides, I wouldn't get all of you and all your luggage into one of those old cabs.'

Sealed With a Kiss

It was a lovely sunny day so Roger and Anne had gone for a ride to the top of a nearby hill.

'Anne,' Roger said, as they stood looking at the view, 'there is something I would like to ask you.' She raised her eyebrows in enquiry as he took her hands in his.

'We've known each other for absolutely ages now but only in the last few weeks have we been close, so this might seem a bit sudden to you.

'However, it's been long enough for me to realise that I'm in love with you. I want to spend the rest of my life with you and I would be very honoured if you would consent to be my wife.'

There was a sharp intake of breath by Anne who had not been expecting this quite so soon.

'Oh yes please, Roger. I'm in love with you, too, and I have been for quite a while

now. Nothing would make me happier.'
She pulled his head down for a long kiss.

'Shall we take the horses back and go
to see your father?' Roger asked eventually.

'By all means, but I can tell you now it
will only be a formality,' Anne said.

They returned to Westwood Hall
where they exchanged their horses for
the Daimler. Roger ran up to his room,
changed quickly and then went down to
the drawing room, where he was sure
to find his father reading the morning
papers as usual.

'Father, I'm taking Miss Harper home
in the Daimler. It's almost noon. I doubt
I shall be back before lunch.'

His father peered over the top of his
newspaper and nodded before returning
to his reading.

Roger hurried back outside where
Anne was waiting for him in the car.

'Everything all right?' she asked.

'Yes, I didn't come across Mother so
she didn't have a chance to invite us both
for lunch. We can join her for tea when

we get back.'

Half an hour later the car drew to a halt outside Anne's house. As Roger went around the car to open the door for Anne, the front door was opened by Johnson the butler.

'Good afternoon, miss. Good afternoon, sir.'

'Johnson, where might we find my father?'

'Sir John is in his study, miss.'

'Would you ask him if he can spare me a few minutes?' Roger asked.

'Certainly, sir,' Johnson said as he went to hang their coats and hats in the hall closet before then moving on to the study.

As they waited for him to come back, Anne bit her lower lip as she fidgeted nervously, trying not to grin. She straightened Roger's tie with trembling fingers.

'Sir John will see you now, sir, if you would follow me, please.'

'I'll get changed while you're speaking to him,' Anne said, before rushing upstairs.

Roger followed the butler to the study.

'Mr Roger Radfield to see you, Sir John.' The butler closed the door softly behind Roger.

'Roger,' Sir John came forward to shake Roger's hand. 'What can I do for you?'

'Well, Sir John, I'll not beat about the bush. You know my family, you know me and I would very much like to marry Anne.'

'Gosh. Well. Yes. That is straight to the point,' Sir John said with a chuckle. He looked at Roger in a considering way. 'I'm happy to give my permission — provided it's not a long-winded, drawn-out engagement.' He raised an eyebrow in query.

'Oh no, sir,' Roger replied, understanding the reference to Anne's previous engagement to James. 'Certainly not. In fact we would like the banns to be read starting next Sunday with a view to a marriage in four weeks' time. That's if the vicar can manage it.'

'Good! Excellent! Stay for lunch?'

'We'd be delighted to, but we mustn't take too long over it as we have to head back to Westwood Hall to tell my parents.'

After lunch, Roger and Anne returned to Westwood Hall. There they found his parents taking tea on the terrace.

'Roger, oh, and Anne,' Lady Radfield said, looking puzzled. 'I thought you had taken Anne home?'

'I did, but only because I needed to speak to Sir John. Once I had, and he had given me permission, I asked Anne to marry me and she accepted.'

His mother's eyes grew round with surprise.

'Marry? Oh how wonderful!' She stepped forward to hug Anne while Roger went to shake his father's hand.

'Have you thought about when you want to have the wedding?'

'We stopped to see the vicar on the way here and he will read the banns on Sunday and so we provisionally booked the church for about four weeks from now.'

'Lady Radfield, I wonder, since my mother is longer with us, would you mind helping me to plan the wedding? My sister is too far away and busy with her children and I doubt my father has much idea of what to do.'

'Mind? Mind? My dear, I will be absolutely delighted. With two sons and no daughters, I've never had a chance to plan a wedding. There is nothing I would like more. Four weeks, you say? Oh, goodness me, that is no time at all, we must get started.

'Come to my sitting-room, we'll make a list of everything that needs to be done.' She hurried off back into the house. Anne, with a shrug and a grin at Roger, followed her.

'You've made me very happy, Roger, partly because you've made your mother ecstatic,' his father said. 'You had better go and tell James so that he knows to keep out of their way for the next month.'

Roger nodded and headed off to the estate office where he found James adding figures in a ledger.

'James, I've just asked Anne to marry me and she's agreed. I hope you're comfortable with this?'

James put his pen down, straightened up with a smile and reached out to shake his brother's hand.

'Comfortable? Good gracious, yes, I am very happy for you both. If anything I'm relieved. I felt a bit uneasy about letting everyone down by breaking the engagement, even though Anne said she wanted to break it, too. I would always have wondered a little bit if she was just saying it out of kindness. Now I've seen the two of you together I'm absolutely sure it was the right thing to do.'

'I'm very glad of that. I wouldn't have wanted you to think I had stolen your fiancée. I'm hoping you'll be my best man.'

'I will be honoured. When's the wedding?'

'Four weeks' time, more or less.'

'Four weeks? Is that long enough for the ladies to get everything ready?'

'Our mother and Anne have already

gone off to Mother's sitting-room to start planning for it.'

'In that case, I have a good bottle of a single malt whisky and a couple of glasses in a drawer and we should stay well out of their way.'

Depressing News

It was definitely autumn and a distinct chill was now present in the rather cloudy and damp weather. Roger and Anne had been married for a month and were back from a honeymoon on the French Riviera.

The Prestons would be settled in Cambridge by now and so Lady Radfield concluded that it was time that she made her promised visit to them.

Lord and Lady Radfield had given Roger and Anne the stud farm as a wedding gift and were having a house built there for them. In the meantime Roger and Anne were living at Westwood Hall.

'Anne,' Lady Radfield said at breakfast, 'I thought to go and see the Prestons in Cambridge today. Would you like to come? Then afterwards we could have lunch in the centre of town and do a little shopping.'

Lady Radfield was well aware that

Anne was finding time hanging heavy on her hands, as she no longer had her father's house to run and Westwood Hall was not hers to run either.

'That sounds like a splendid idea. Perhaps we could look around some furniture stores for the new house.'

By mid-morning, they were at the Prestons' house and the chauffeur was ringing the door bell for them. Moments later the door was opened by Mrs Preston.

'Lady Radfield!' she exclaimed in surprise. 'How nice to see you, do come in.' Mrs Preston was privately relieved that she had chosen to wear one of her better dresses that morning, in anticipation of the Methodist mothers meeting that afternoon.

Lady Radfield and Anne stepped into the hallway.

'I do hope it is not inconvenient,' Lady Radfield said, 'but we were coming to the shops in Cambridge and we couldn't come without calling to see you.'

'Not at all, we're delighted to see you,

it's perfectly convenient. The Reverend is working in his study and I'll let him know you're here. In the meantime, do go into the parlour and take a seat,' she said, ushering them through one of the doors, 'and I'll make some tea.'

At this point the Reverend emerged from his study having heard the voices in the hall.

'Lady Radfield, good morning, how nice to see you again.'

'Good morning, Reverend,' she replied, shaking his hand. 'I think you've met my daughter-in-law Anne on one occasion before, haven't you?'

'Yes, I remember,' he replied and shook Anne's hand too. 'We met briefly in Ipswich when you came to collect James. Do come into the parlour and tell me how he is getting on.'

They chatted for half an hour over tea and biscuits before the Radfield ladies left for the shops in the centre of town. Somehow, in that time, it never became apparent that Anne had married Roger rather than James.

Margaret came home in time for lunch, having been to the library. As she was removing her coat, the kitchen door opened and she could smell the aromas of lunch as her stepmother carried a dish to the dining-room.

'Ah, you're back. You've just missed Lady Radfield and her daughter-in-law Anne.'

Margaret's thoughts immediately went to James, despite her best efforts for weeks to not think of him again.

'How is James? Is he well?'

'Yes, they said he was fully recovered. They're building a new house in the grounds of Westwood Hall for the newly-weds and they came into Cambridge to look for furniture for it. It was kind of them to call.'

'Yes, it was.' Margaret was not especially surprised by the news, it was after all, what she had expected, but nevertheless it still left her feeling more upset than she cared to admit.

220

She had thought herself resigned to the situation, but she later spent a gloomy afternoon darning a pair of woollen gloves and trying not to dwell on the depressing news that James and Anne were now married.

Christmas Shopping

Christmas was approaching and Margaret was musing about suitable gifts for her father and stepmother. For her new stepmother something for the kitchen probably wouldn't work, since her stepmother had probably seen and done everything there was to do in a kitchen.

Eventually Margaret hit upon the idea of books. Perhaps something studious for her father like a history of Cambridge and something lighter for her stepmother. A romance where the housekeeper marries the widowed lord of the house might be amusing if she could find such a theme.

Cambridge was very well endowed with bookshops, primarily for the students and other academics, but the shelves were by no means full only of serious topics.

Margaret put on her hat, scarf, coat and gloves, collected her handbag and put her head into the study to tell her father she was going shopping.

She smiled at his mumbled and absent.minded acknowledgement before walking down the street and across the river bridge into the centre of town. Grey clouds were speeding across the sky and a chill wind was making her face cold, so she walked briskly to keep warm.

As she hadn't lived long in Cambridge, she still had only a slight familiarity with all the bookshops, so she went to Heffer's bookshop in Petty Cury which she knew was the largest.

Margaret was grateful to get into the shop, not that it was particularly warm, but at least it was out of the biting wind. The bookshop was very big with rows and rows of tall bookcases, whose dark brown colour gave the shop a gloomy appearance, even though it was actually well lit.

From the front of the bookshop, it was difficult to see all the way to the back. Since the bookshelves were taller than the customers, one had the impression that the shop was almost empty, as hardly anybody was visible unless one was looking down the aisle between shelves.

Margaret supposed that each day at closing time the staff had to check the shop thoroughly so as to not lock an absent minded and unseen customer inside.

Because this was such a large bookshop, she was optimistic that she might find here both books for which she was searching. The romantic novel for her stepmother was likely to be the easiest to find so she decided to look for that first and an assistant directed her to shelves to one side and towards the back of the shop. She was soon completely engrossed in browsing through dozens of titles.

The Greatest Gift of All

James had also been puzzling over what gift he might buy for his parents. He too thought a book for his father might be appropriate. Whilst Newmarket might be a good place to look for a history of horse racing or horse breeding, he thought his mother might prefer something more fragrant and fictional than yet another volume to do with horses.

Accordingly a trip to Cambridge was in order and after stepping off the train at Cambridge station he took the green Ortona Company bus into the centre of town and to the stop in St Andrew's Street.

The nearest bookshop was Heffer's in Petty Cury, so not surprisingly he walked into the very same bookshop as Margaret had done a short while before. As he went in he paused and surveyed the very large maze of bookshelves. He blew his cheeks out. Where to start?

'Excuse me,' he said to a young shop girl filling a bookshelf, 'where might I find light novels suitable for an older lady?'

'Three rows over, sir,' she said, pointing, 'and then towards the back of the shop you will find romantic fiction. Could this be what you had in mind?'

'Thank you, yes, I shall take a look,' James replied and headed the way she had indicated. As he walked slowly along the ends of the bookshelves, he read the topics painted on the ends of shelves.

When he reached the third one, reassuringly labelled 'Fiction', he turned into the aisle to see what he could find. As he inspected the shelves he realised this was all kinds of fiction and recalled the assistant had said to go towards the back of the shop.

He turned away from the shelves to face down the row and suddenly realised that there was something very familiar about the lady examining the books at the other end of the row. He looked carefully down the slightly gloomy aisle and slowly walked closer. The lady had a coat with a high collar and a warm hat down to her ears, but there could be no doubt.

'Margaret!' he exclaimed.

Margaret had been browsing through the books on the Romance shelf and, being absorbed in her task, was paying no attention to the shop assistants and other customers wandering around the bookshop. She started as she heard her name and looked around. A broad smile filled her face as she spotted James coming towards her.

'James, what a surprise! I didn't expect to see you here.'

James walked between the remaining bookshelves to where Margaret was standing.

'Well, equally, I never expected to see you . . . er, here,' James very nearly said that he had never expected to see her ever again, but he caught himself in time.

'Are you well?' he asked rather lamely.

'Yes, I'm very well,' she said, clasping her trembling hands. 'But what about you? I heard you got hit on the head again.'

'Oh, yes. It was a disaffected soldier who lost an arm in the war and his job afterwards. I'm afraid he blamed me for all his woes.'

'Do you suppose it was the same man as in Ipswich?'

'More than likely, but I suspect he had a two-armed accomplice then and I also suspect I know who that was, but I can't prove anything. At least this time I wasn't hit so hard and didn't lose my memory.'

'You mustn't joke about it, it would have been truly awful a second time. Are you really well?'

'Oh, I'm fine,' James said, holding his hat in his hands and fiddling nervously with its brim. 'I'm looking for books as Christmas presents for my parents.'

'How very odd,' she replied, tilting her head slightly to one side, 'that's exactly what I'm doing too!'

There was a pause as they both studied each other, smiles creeping on to their faces. James knew he couldn't just turn and walk away, but uncharacteristically he felt nervous and unsure what to do.

He knew that she was married now and beyond his reach, but a short chat with an old friend was allowed, wasn't it? And a little happiness had to be better than nothing, but it didn't have to be in a bookshop for only a few brief moments before they both moved on, did it?

'Would you like to join me for a coffee?' James asked. 'You can tell me what has been happening since we last saw each other.' As soon as he said that, James knew he was a fool. He was just going to hear about her wedding and married life and it would twist the knife in his heart. But he just couldn't help himself.

'Thank you, I would love a coffee,' she said. 'There's a Lyons Tea Shop a few doors away, will that do?'

'It sounds splendid. You obviously know where it is, so please lead the way,' he said, as he stepped to the side and invited her to go in front of him.

James followed Margaret out of the

bookshop and into the nearby tea shop where they took a corner table. Nothing was said on the way except for a few speaking glances and slightly nervous smiles. They put their hats and coats on the spare chairs and when the Nippy arrived, James ordered coffee for two.

For James, Margaret's marriage was like an insect bite on his soul. It itched and he knew he shouldn't scratch it but sometimes you just couldn't stop yourself.

'How is Ian?'

Margaret was clearly a little surprised. She straightened, frowned a moment and then raised her eyebrows slightly.

'As far as I know, he's well but I haven't seen him for quite some time.'

It was now James's turn to be surprised.

'Are you here on a long visit to your father then?'

Margaret's reply was delayed as the Nippy put the coffee jug, cups, sugar bowl and cream on their table.

'No,' she said slowly, 'I'm not visiting,

I live here in Cambridge now.'

James knew he was missing something. He wondered what it was as Margaret poured the coffee. She didn't ask if he took cream or sugar; she knew from before in Ipswich. What did she mean 'quite some time'? Was this hours, days or weeks? Perhaps the good doctor was travelling for some reason.

'Is Ian still in Ipswich or did he move here, too?'

'Well naturally he's still in Ipswich, he's a partner in the doctor's surgery there. I can't imagine him moving here,' Margaret said, now regarding James with a puzzled expression on her face.

James sipped thoughtfully at his coffee. He wasn't going to work this out without asking a blunt question.

'I know it's none of my business, so I shouldn't really ask, but didn't the marriage work out for some reason?'

'I don't understand,' Margaret said, sitting back in her chair. 'What marriage do you mean?'

'Your marriage to Ian.'

'I didn't marry Ian. I refused his offer.' Margaret stared blankly at James, wondering why he thought she had married Ian.

James felt a momentary elation and then stopped and thought about what had been said for a moment.

'But, wait a minute. When my mother and I visited your father in Ipswich he said that you were on honeymoon in Brighton following your wedding.'

Margaret thought over this for a few moments then she laughed.

'Oh no! You obviously misunderstood what he said. Yes, it was correct that I was in Brighton for a fortnight but staying with an aunt, not on honeymoon. My father married our housekeeper, Mrs Hodges as was, and I went to Brighton for two weeks to give them some time on their own.'

Margaret knew those decisions had been right. She was happy with her new stepmother and had no real regrets about refusing Ian. Her only regret was losing the man sitting in front of her and she couldn't help that.

James was dumbfounded and sat back in his own chair, blinking as he thought it over.

'So all this time when I thought you were married to Ian and living in Ipswich you were actually living in Cambridge with your father and a new stepmother?'

'Absolutely correct,' Margaret said, grinning. 'If your brother hadn't collected you so early on that Saturday morning you would have known all about it.'

James cursed under his breath; so much agony all for nothing and so much time wasted. Now he knew he didn't want to waste any further time to win the woman he loved. He sat forward and clasped Margaret's hand as it rested on the table.

'So if you're still single, perhaps I could call on you?'

Margaret stiffened and pulled her hand away.

'I'm sorry, James,' she said with all trace of a grin now gone. 'I'm not that kind of girl. I think perhaps I should leave now.' She picked up her handbag and coat and prepared to rise from the table.

'Wait, wait!' James said, thoroughly alarmed and wondering what he said wrong. 'I don't understand, why not?'

'Why not?' Margaret said in an angry and disgusted tone of voice. 'Because you're a married man and should know better. I'm sorry, but I shouldn't even have joined you for coffee.' Margaret stood up.

'But I'm not married!' James blurted out as he stood as well.

'James, please don't lie to me,' Margaret said angrily, but keeping her voice down. 'Your mother visited my parents with Anne, who was your fiancée, and introduced her as her daughter-in-law so I know you're married.' Margaret turned away to walk to the door.

'But she married Roger, not me!' a distressed James said loudly. He was desperate now and didn't care if the other people in the coffee house were looking around to see what was going on. Having just found that the love of his life was free and unmarried he didn't want to lose her again.

Margaret paused as she considered what he had said. She remembered her first impressions at that dance in Ipswich. She turned back to James.

'Anne married Roger?' she said, more quietly than before.

'Yes, Anne married Roger, not me,' James said, reaching for Margaret's hand and drawing her back to the table. 'Anne realised that she didn't want to marry me and I knew I didn't want to marry her because I was really in love with you.'

They didn't realise, because James and Margaret were now totally focused on each other, but their loud voices had attracted the full attention of the suddenly quiet coffee house. Even the waitresses serving the tables had paused with bated breath to see what would happen next.

'You love me?' Margaret squeaked, wondering if she had heard correctly.

'Yes, I love you with all my heart. Ever since I met you, you have been constantly in my thoughts. I love you so much that when I thought you loved Ian, all I wanted was your happiness and so I could say nothing when he asked you to marry him.

'I have never stopped loving you and the thought of never seeing you again was agony. Yes, I do love you and I'm desperately hoping you might love me too

— if not now then some day,' James said, impetuously pulling her close so that he could kiss her.

She didn't resist. The way that she put her arms around his neck and pulled him closer for a fierce kiss made James feel that maybe she did feel something after all and that just maybe all would be right with the world.

They broke the kiss but stayed holding each other tightly.

'Oh James, I do love you. I have done since the beginning,' Margaret said breathlessly, her eyes moist with joy.

There was simply only one more thing that James could wish for on this glorious day.

'Marry me?' he asked.

236

'Oh yes!' Margaret replied without hesitation and pulled him back for another enthusiastic kiss.

There was a collective sigh in the coffee house as the spectators let out the breath they had been holding, followed by clapping and cheering.

James and Margaret broke the kiss on hearing the applause and looked around in amazement. They had been totally lost to the rest of the world and had completely forgotten where they were. They had certainly had not realised they were the focus of attention of the whole coffee shop.

'I think it's time we drank our coffee, I paid the bill and we went for a walk,' James said sheepishly. 'A very long walk. We have an awful lot to talk about.'

Other titles in the
Linford Romance Library:

WINGS OF A NIGHTINGALE

Alan C. Williams

It's 1941 when strong-willed Aussie nurse, Pauline Newton, arrives at Killymoor Hall, a British military hospital which has many secrets. Most crucially, it's a base for a team of Nazi saboteurs. Falling in love with the mysterious Sergeant Ray Tennyson, Pauline finds herself involved in murders, skulduggery and intrigue as they both race desperately to discover the German leaders' identity. Throughout it all, Ray and Pauline must resolve their own differences if they hope to stop the Nazis altering the War's outcome forever.

MURDER IN THE HAUNTED CASTLE

Ken Preston

Divorced Kim has come to terms with the fact that her only daughter is growing up. A last memorable holiday together before Maddie immerses herself in GCSE revision seems just the thing. But as if meeting the delectable James (no, not Bond — but close!) isn't exciting enough to throw a spanner in the works, just wait until they all get to the haunted castle. Dream holiday? More like a nightmare! But how will it end ... ?

ISLAND OF MISTS

Evelyn Orange

Arasay — remote Scottish island, wildlife haven, and home to Jenna's ancestors. When she arrives to help out her great aunt in the bookshop, she's running from her past and hiding from the world. But she's not expecting to meet an attractive wildlife photographer who is also using the island to escape from previous traumas. As Jenna embraces island life and becomes closer to Jake and his family, there are secrets in the mist that could threaten their future happiness . . .